# THE S..... TEEN

*The Ultimate Guide*
*to Social Skills for Teens*

Build Unstoppable Confidence, Create Healthy Boundaries, Overcome Anxiety (and Other Emotional Monsters), Make Great Friends, Emotional Regulation, Time Management and Other Awesome Life Skills

# CONTENTS

# *Introduction*
## WHAT'S IN HERE?

**Before we take the first step, I want you to understand how unique, talented, and amazing you actually are.** Whether you are told this or not, I want you to know this is an absolute fact. Everyone goes through moments in their life when we forget this or never even realize our own light. Even when you may not be getting this from the outside world, just know the huge possibilities within you, but you have to learn how to flick that light on and keep it on! This book will teach you life-changing skills that will make your life happier, more fulfilling, and filled with purpose. **I want to share this with you because THIS is the book I wish I had as a teen navigating through the years of toxic comparisons, friends, family and school pressures, anxiety, insecurities, and my own internal thoughts. I've been there. And the reality is, these skills aren't just for the teen years. These are life long skills that I wish someone had mapped out to me at your age and why I think it is so important you learn these skills early.**

Think of the concept of these skills like a trajectory in science class. **In the beginning, the impact may be small but as you get older the impact will get bigger and bigger as you manage life in college, career and family....and I want your future world to be as open and wide as possible.**

**I have also included some self-reflective workbook questions to drill down WHO you are so you can get to who you want to be.** And don't worry, this isn't going to add to all the other stuff you got going on, in case you were thinking that. I know the last thing you want is MORE homework after you went to school all day, ran to after-school stuff, and then did your regular homework. I know by that time, you are just burnt. I don't want to add to your workload. Just write what feels comfortable. But I will say that you may have to just think deeply about some of the questions to make sure they come from your heart. This can require you to take some time to look at a question and then think about it for a bit to get to an answer that's your truth, and that's perfectly fine.

You will learn how knowing who you are will step up your self-confidence and open up your world to more friends and stronger relationships. You will uncover your unique talents and learn why growing them makes you happier, how to overcome anxiety, and not let other emotional monsters take the wheel. You will also learn steps to better handle brain-freezing stress and time management. Finally...this is a big one...mindset. You will learn how to change the esteem bashing negative self-talk into grounding supportive and confident self-talk and breakdown the walls of your limiting beliefs.

Navigating through the teen years can be tough for everyone, even IF people seem like they have it easy and don't show it to the world. You have a ton of changes, challenges, and growth coming at you from all angles, and it's completely normal to feel overwhelmed at times. **That's why I want this book to be like a heart-to-heart talk with your most understanding and wisest friend, someone who truly gets you. My intention is not to lecture you but rather to provide you with real tips, advice, and strategies to make your journey through these important life-changing years smoother, more fulfilling and fun.**

I'm here to help you find out exactly who you are, how to develop unshakable confidence, make real friends, overcome emotional obstacles, manage stress and an overwhelming schedule, set healthy boundaries, communicate better, speak up effectively, and other super important skills that not only will help you through these the teens years but build a base for the rest of your life.

So, let's get to it and figure this out together!

# Chapter One
## WHO ARE YOU?

*"Knowing yourself is the beginning of all wisdom."*
— *Aristotle*

I remember when I was seven years old, just being young and not really thinking about what people thought of me, my self-image, and life pressures. I was going about living life in my own 7-year-old clueless bubble of family, fighting with my sister, friends, school, being who I was, and finding out kid ways to entertain myself.

Then BOOM. When I turned 11, life started to change fast. My feelings got more complex. There were lots and lots of thoughts floating around in my head constantly. I started spending hours in the mirror worrying about how I looked. Am I pretty? Am I pretty enough? What IS that on my face? Do people think I'm smart? Am I too short? I'm really upset, but should I be? Why do I feel like this? Is this fair? How do I say this? Is this cool? Do they like me? What are they thinking about me? Why am I so weird? I didn't want to feel different because that's weird. I just wanted to be like everyone else. I started to really compare myself to other people in a way I didn't before. I felt like I was a little different and thought differently, but does everyone feel like that?

**YES! Some are better at hiding it than others.** You probably look around and see some people have zero problem fitting in. You see them. Life seems easier for them on the outside. You wish you had it that easy and have it all figured out. What I want to tell you is that everyone goes through the same internal weirdness and questions that you go through.

You just never FULLY know someone else's journey and what goes on in their lives and heads. **And MOST of what people think about themselves, they never ever talk about...and you never see it.** Most will want to keep up that "I'm doing great" front. But every single one of us has our own "moments" of feeling insecure, not sure of ourselves, not feeling perfect, not fully fitting in...that we never show to the outside world. Or if we do, then we only share this stuff with a tiny group of trusted people.

Does this sound familiar? So, I want you to know you are not alone. You don't need to be fixed, and there is nothing wrong with you. The YOU that you don't want to stick out so much is the YOU that you are actually meant to be.

Let me explain. The part of you that is different and the journey this takes you on is the exact part of you that is so valuable. The part of you that feels different is what makes you so special. So don't try to squish it down and out because it's the you that the world needs. It's the YOU that makes you a great friend, a great person, and completely unique. You just may need some help letting all that good stuff inside you out. But it's already in there!

This chapter starts out by asking a very important question.. "who ARE you"? You are probably thinking, "What does that mean, and **why does it matter**"? Let me explain why this is probably one of the most important questions you can ask yourself. **It's simply because you can't be confident if you really don't know WHO you are!** Let's get into this deeper...what do you like or not like, what are your values, what do you believe in, etc.? This is the type of stuff you are going to find out about yourself to get down to figuring out WHO you are.

And let me rephrase this so you get me. **You WILL be more confident if you take the time to figure out who you really are.** I'm not talking about the fake confidence you can bring out when you are at a party smiling, but inside, you feel completely out of place and awkward hoping no one can read it from your face. And some of us fake that really well.

I'm talking about real confidence that comes from deep inside. The type of confidence that you can always get to if something shakes you up. The kind of confidence that you always know, "I'm OK," "I got this," or "I feel confident enough in myself to ask for help," or "this is what I need".

Knowing the answers to what makes you YOU and what you believe in and understanding how you think will help be a guide when life starts to test you. Now you have some understanding of why this question is important and how it will have a big impact on your self-confidence.

Your next question probably is, "How do I find out who I am"? Finding out who you are takes some quiet time to ask your specific questions with full, straight-up honesty.

You may not have even REALLY asked yourself who you are before because you may not have realized how huge this question was. **But knowing who you are is the start of where everything grows from.**

The starting point to answering this question is, really asking first, who do you "think" you are. I don't mean who your friends think you are, or your parents think you are, or your teachers think you are. **Who do YOU think you are? To start off, how do you SEE yourself?** Do you see yourself as smart, athletic, good-looking, funny, etc.?

**Let's go through your image of how YOU see yourself:**

Smart, artistic, great at music, pretty, cute, beautiful, handsome, outgoing, introverted, nice, mean, athletic, kind, generous, selfish, average looking, not attractive, not smart, overweight, popular, not popular, funny, brave, fearful, leader, follower, organized, quiet, loud, hyper, a fabulous dresser, creative, trouble-maker, peace-keeper, strong, weak, lazy, hard worker, overachiever, misunderstood, easy going, hard to get along with, emotional, calm, friendly, shy, unreliable, dependable.

_____

_____

_____

_____

_____

**Think of some other words you want to add to the list that are not there. Circle all the things YOU think you are.**

**Now, take a look at everything you circled or wrote.** Look at all the words that make you feel like you are "not enough" of something. The reason I bring this up is for two reasons:

1.  **If people were really being honest, MOST of the time, people think of themselves as "less than" something, not "more than" something.** This is everyone. In fact, most people have to psych themselves up and work to think of themselves as "more than." This is because our brain just NATURALLY falls to "less than." Again, as I mentioned before, **pretty much everyone never talks about what they are actually thinking about themselves.** Yes, that goes for the person in class who seems to have everything together. These ideas about ourselves are just cloud thoughts that float around in our brains that are never heard or fully formed. This is why I want you to write it down, circle it, and really look at all the words YOU think describe you.

2.  **The second reason is, many times our view of ourselves is NOT REAL.** This is the reason why it's a problem. **What we THINK of**

ourselves directly impacts how we ACT and SPEAK. I would say how we view ourselves is probably the most important thing we can be aware of. If there is one statement to take away from this book, it is that...HOW WE VIEW OURSELVES IS THE MOST IMPORTANT THING WE CAN BE AWARE OF.

Why? YOU USUALLY BECOME HOW YOU THINK YOU ARE. If you don't think you are smart, you may not shoot for the A because you think, "Why bother? I'm not the smart kid. I can't do it". You may not study as hard because a C or D is fine because that's the best you think your brain can get.

If you think you are unreliable, you will probably keep mismanaging time, breaking promises, and missing deadlines because it fits what you think of yourself anyway. **But I'm telling you, it doesn't have to be that way.**

**And more importantly, it won't be that way if you do the work and learn the skills in this book and make them into a habit...something you do every day.** Even if you get sidetracked sometimes that's OK and normal. But when you get sidetracked or distracted, get right back to it again. **That's how something becomes a habit.** When things become a habit, it goes on autopilot, which just means you start doing it naturally and with less effort than you needed when you first started. You still need effort but less to muster up when you started this whole process.

A habit isn't formed overnight and just takes repetition and practice. **Studies show it takes about 30 days of doing something every day to make something a habit.** If 30 days seems too long for you to commit to right now, just start with one week and take it from there. **Taking lots of baby steps consistently to achieve a big goal makes it much more attainable than taking fewer big steps to achieve that same big goal.** Got it?

This takes time, but I promise you your life will be better because of it. Remember, If you really know who you are and what you are really able to do, then life becomes happier, and more things open up for you.

And let me tell you a secret. Even most adults do not know who they are and what they are capable of. **I want you to learn these skills at a young age so you can really flourish in your teen years and beyond.** So, what I want you to do is rethink who you are and how you see yourself.

Take from the above exercise of who you THINK you list of "not enough" ones. Cross them out and put the opposite in its place. Even cross out the ones that are "average intelligence." Put in its place "smart". You are not ordinary or average. **I want you to look at the "not enough" list turned into "more than enough" list daily. Put them up near your mirror or someplace you can see them every day.** You got it? That's the 1st step. Look at your new "more than" list. **Learn to see yourself differently every day. Again, make this a habit.**

**The next step in finding out who you are is…what else is in there?** Let's find out more about what makes you tick. What do you like and not like, what you are passionate about, what bothers you? What's important to you? What makes you happy?

**This is not a list of what you are SUPPOSED to like or not like, etc. This is about you and your truth.** That's what we are here to find out. These are all questions so you can get to know yourself better!

Remember, there are no wrong answers here. I want you to be free to write down what is in your mind and heart. **I want you to learn the important skill of asking yourself targeted questions so you understand yourself better.** If it's hard to find your answers, then the best thing is to write it down!

**Writing is the BEST way to get clear on what you are thinking!** Once you start writing down how you think, feel, like, what bothers you, what's important to you, basically, putting actual words to your thoughts and feelings, you have opened the door to open up the real you.

**When you see it printed in front of you, you start getting clear what you are about!** If you start getting clear about what you are about, then you get to know who you are. **If you start getting to know who you are, you start building self-confidence because you don't feel like you are floating around and struggling to figure out what you want.** If you get more confident, then you are able to make new connections easier, overcome fears, speak up, and create healthy boundaries. You see where I'm going with this? **It all starts with getting to know who you are and knowing that everything that makes up YOU is a gift.**

This process of asking yourself questions may seem silly at first, but I want you to get into the habit of asking yourself straight up what you think, feel, and believe about things regularly. This will help you get clear. **Again, when you get clear, it becomes easier to find direction. When you get direction, then your actions can become more focused and effective to get the results you want.**

So, let's keep this rolling. The following questions ask you about what you like/love/are drawn to and sometimes why. You may not even know WHY you like something, but if you ask yourself these types of questions, then you can get a better understanding of yourself.

You can fill these answers out at your own pace. You can always go back to them. Again, this shouldn't feel like additional homework and obligations. **These are just some questions to get to know yourself better in print and gain insight.**

What type of music are you into?

_____

_____

How does the music make you feel?

_____

_____

What artists do you love?

_____

_____

What is it about them that you connect with?

_____

_____

_____

What sports do you love to watch?

_____

_____

Why do you like those sports versus others?

_____

_____

_____

**Which sports do you love to play? What positions are you great at?**

_____

_____

**Why do you love to play this/these sports, and how does it make you feel?**

_____

_____

_____

_____

**What are your all-time favorite movies?**

_____

_____

**Why are they so special to you?**

_____

_____

_____

_____

**Do you have a favorite director? If so, who?**

_____

_____

**Why do you think this director is so special?**

_____

_____

_____

**What are your favorite hobbies?**

_____

_____

**Why did these hobbies become your favorites?**

_____

_____

_____

**What are your favorite subjects at school?**

_____

_____

**What do you like about these subjects?**

_____

_____

_____

**Think of some other questions you want to ask yourself below and answer them.**

**QUESTION:**

_____

**ANSWER:**

_____

_____

Let's start thinking about the larger questions...

Are there any problems in the world you want to fix and why?

_____

_____

_____

_____

Are there some things you want to do or try that you haven't?

_____

_____

Why do you want to try them?

_____

_____

_____

What makes you REALLY happy?

_____

_____

_____

**What other things do you like to do and think you are good at?**

_____

_____

_____

**Is there something you like to do that really lights you up? How does that make you feel?**

_____

_____

_____

_____

## ▌ VALUES

Now, let's talk about values. What exactly are values? **Values are the principles that are important to you. They guide how we live, make decisions, and interact with other people.** Think of them like the guidelines you follow in your life because they feel right to you.

They shape your character. What is character, by the way? Well, it is what makes you YOU. For example, when someone asks, "What is he/she/they all about?" or "What type of person is he/she/they?" they are asking about character. Are they reliable, kind, hard-working, tries to make everyone laugh and have fun? They are describing your character.

VALUES are part of your character and help you figure out what's important to YOU, what's right and wrong, and how to treat others. Examples of values include honesty, respect, kindness, fairness, responsibility, and courage. **Each person's values can be different, and our values influence the choices we make in life and how we view our world.**

So...to put it simply, values are inner beliefs that guide your actions. **Think of them like a personal GPS for navigating life.** Values are the inner compass that help you decide what's important to you and what you stand for. **So, when life throws hurdles your way and tries to confuse you, your values are the rock-solid beliefs that help you stay true to who you are and what you believe in.** They are beliefs that are really important to you and that you may choose as a priority.

**What do you think some of your values are? Here are some examples.**

**Respect** = Treating others, as well as yourself, with consideration and dignity.

**Kindness** = Being compassionate and considerate when dealing with others.

**Integrity** = Being honest, truthful, true to yourself, and doing the right thing.

**Responsibility** = Own up to your actions and your obligations.

**Empathy** = Understanding the feelings of others. Basically, the ability to see something in someone else's shoes and show you care.

**Courage** = Facing challenges (even though you may even be afraid) with bravery and determination.

**Perseverance** = Staying committed, grinding, and pushing through to your goals even though there are difficulties.

**Honesty** = Being truthful and straight up with what you say and do.

**Gratitude** = Appreciating all the good in your life (big and small) and saying thanks with real sincerity (not just because you have to, because it is polite or someone tells you to).

**Humility** = Staying humble (not bragging about everything), knowing your strengths, weaknesses, and learning from experiences.

**Self-Respect** = Love and value yourself, own your uniqueness and who you are. Stand up for yourself when you need to.

**Generosity** = Being willing to share, whether it's your time, kindness, or what you have with others. Basically, share the love.

**Friendship/relationships** = Prioritizing your people, your friends, having their backs, and all around being a really good friend.

**Inclusive** = Open to differences and make sure everyone feels included.

**Optimism** = Staying positive and looking for the good in situations (even the tough ones).

**Curiosity** = Being open-minded, exploring, and learning from new things.

**Creativity** = Expressing yourself in your own way, whether through art, music, ideas, dance, or other innovative ways.

**Independence** = Developing the ability to make your own decisions and choices and owning them.

**Environmental Consciousness** = Taking care of the planet and environment and being eco-friendly

**Teamwork** = Working together with others to get things done.

**Justice** = Wanting to stand up for what is right and make sure people are treated as fairly and equally as possible.

There are some of the values that you may be drawn to that are not on the list, like hard-working, being helpful, staying true to yourself, striving for excellence, self-care, having fun, and having balance can also be on the list. You may even think of some of your own.

**Write down the values that mean the most to you.**

---

_____

_____

_____

_____

## WHY DO YOU CHOOSE ONE PRIORITY OVER ANOTHER?

Whether you realize it or not, our personal values directly influence what we do and what we choose. Discovering what your core values are makes a really powerful impact because they can help you figure out what internal guidance system you are ALREADY using in your life when you make decisions.

For example, say one of your core values is justice. You see someone getting bullied. This really upsets you, so you get right up in the bully's face and defend the person being bullied. **That is your value system kicking in and you may not have even known it.** There are other people around seeing the exact same thing but many of them are just watching and standing there. Your reaction is to stand up to the bully because you can't stand when you see someone getting mistreated. Your values drive your actions all the time.

There are some scenarios too where there can be a conflict of values and one wins over another in that moment. That could be because a value has a higher ranking than another to you, or the scale of the scenario. Sometimes choosing which value outranks another is an easy choice or a hard choice.

For example, some of your core values are having fun, friendship, and empathy. Say that you had plans to go to a fun event with your family that night, but your friend was having a terrible time with something going on in his/her/their life and really needed a friend to talk to. Since friendship and empathy may be a bigger priority for you than having fun AT THAT MOMENT, you tell your family you think it is best if you hang with your friend and be supportive. You see, we make decisions based on our value system constantly.

In this scenario, it wasn't as if your "family" and "having fun" values weren't important to you. But the "having fun" with your family value seemed smaller than your friend needing someone he/she/they could trust to talk to about something that was really upsetting them. **The scale of the scenario plays a big part as well.** It is not that having fun isn't important to you because who doesn't like to have fun? But at certain moments, some values are more important than other values.

**Since core values could be the root reasons why you do something,** if you come across decisions and challenges, you can understand yourself better on how and WHY you choose something. You can rearrange your choices, thought processes, and actions more toward your goals if you know what values are important to you.

For example, say that a core value of yours is getting excellent grades (or striving for excellence) and being successful at school. **I am not talking about this being a core value of your parents, your teachers, or your family, but this is an actual core value deep inside of YOU.** If you recognize this as one of your core values, then you will likely choose activities and arrange your schedule around making sure you have enough time to get all your school work done well. This may be saying no to friends sometimes, not going to a game, etc.

**Now, think about what happens if someone doesn't know their core values. It's so easy to get confused and insecure about your decisions if you don't know what is really important to you.** Think how differently you would act if you knew, "This is absolutely important to me." You become more focused and confident about your choices. You recognize it means something to you. That's a core value. If you know your core values ahead of time because you know yourself, then you are less likely to feel confused, directionless, indecisive, and not confident in your decisions. **When your actions align with your core values, you feel a sense of stability, being real with yourself, and become more confident.**

This is why it's really important to examine your values. **They are the guardrails that shape your behavior, decisions, and interactions with the world.** They are deep-rooted beliefs about what is important in your life, what is right and just, and what makes you feel more fulfilled. Also, you can regularly re-evaluate and revisit your core values as your life changes. It just helps to get more clear.

**A value that may be important to you for a couple of years may not be as important as another value later on.**

For example, you are one of five kids, and one of your core values is standing out and making yourself heard. When you are around your siblings, you are loud and do things that will get you noticed because you are part of a big family and don't want to be left in the background. You definitely want to have your say on dinner ideas or other group decisions. As you get older into your teen years, that isn't a big deal to you anymore because you value being independent and doing your own thing more. So you see, values change all the time, **so it is good to be aware of what yours are during a specific time so you realize what is important to you at that moment in your life.**

**Think of a scenario where you easily chose one core value over another? What were the values?**

_____

_____

_____

_____

_____

_____

_____

_____

_____

_____

Now think of a scenario where you had a conflict between two values. What were they?

_____

_____

_____

_____

_____

_____

_____

_____

What are some values that used to be important to you when you were younger, that isn't as important now?

_____

_____

_____

_____

## Chapter Two
# EMBRACE YOUR UNIQUENESS: SHINE YOUR LIGHT

*"Be yourself. Everyone else is taken"*
*— Oscar Wilde*

Remember, I had mentioned in the first section that being different is ACTUALLY a benefit. There are times when everyone feels different and doesn't feel like they fully fit in. But in the unique ways you are and feel different, I want you to understand that this is not only supposed to happen but also to embrace it. You are different because you are MEANT to be different, and that is your superpower. You are unique, and that means **you have something different to offer to the world than anyone else.**

Just like there are no two people ever with the same exact fingerprint, there are no snowflakes that are exactly the same. The same goes with you. There was never anyone in history, currently existing now and there will never be in the future that will ever be just like you. Ever. There will never be anyone with the same mix of ideas, thoughts, looks, and talents who have had the same experiences as you. You are 100% completely unique. It's really an amazing fact, isn't it? **And I want to tell you this is on purpose.** There is no mistake. That means there is no one ever that is better to be you than YOU. **And If you try to be anyone other than who you are, then you run the big risk of not being as happy and as confident because you are not being who you were MEANT to be.**

Many of us grow up ashamed of how we are different when, in fact, our uniqueness will end up being an amazing gift. Here are some examples of how people used their uniqueness as a strength.

## STORY OF ALBERT EINSTEIN

Albert Einstein is one of the most famous scientists that ever existed. He won a Nobel Prize for theoretical physics and contributed significantly to the field by coming up with the theory of relativity and the famous equation E=mc2 (Energy equals mass times the speed of light squared).

While he is most known for his mathematics and physics genius, growing up, he had a lot of difficulties learning in school. He was very slow to talk, didn't speak at all until he was two years old, and didn't fully speak until he was six. He had a lot of problems expressing thoughts, understanding language, and reading. It is now thought he displayed characteristics of dyslexia and autism.

But his so-called "learning disabilities" were not necessarily disabilities but a different way that his mind worked. He could see the world differently and had incredible, innovative problem-solving skills. He often cited his parents as the ones who gave him the belief to embrace his uniqueness, believe in himself, and view his "different" mind as a gift instead of a burden. He was extremely curious and would often look for answers to his questions on his own. Because of this deep-rooted strong sense of self, he was able to spark a completely new segment of science in addition to changing how the world views, religion, unseen forms of energy and even self -help.

## STORY OF LIZZO

**"I think I just kind of started to tear those insecurities down and reclaim the confidence I was born with, my God-given confidence that we all have. I had to make decisions to be patient with myself, to have conversations out loud by myself."**

*— Lizzo*

Lizzo, the award-winning artist the world knows for her amazing talents and empowering messages of confidence, self-love, and resilience, wasn't always so sure of herself. She was once so insecure that she didn't like to perform solo. She didn't see any stars that looked like HER. Every star she saw was thinner and light-skinned, with few exceptions. Even if she felt she was more talented, she didn't think people would want to hear a song coming from her.

She said she had to address every flaw she thought she had and every insecurity and change her mind to view herself as not being ugly but beautiful, unique, and a talent to be heard AND seen. She said AS SOON as she embraced everything different about herself and was kinder to herself, is when her career began to take off.

Now, she is a vocal advocate for issues like body positivity and racial equality and uses her platform to inspire positive change. In a world often shaped by conformity, Lizzo's individuality becomes a light of celebration for diversity, self-expression, and empowerment, making her a special and influential artist. Her unapologetic authenticity, musical talent spanning singing, rapping, and even playing the flute, and the infectious confidence she exudes make her a standout figure. She is being who she is meant to be.

## STORY OF AWKWAFINA

The Korean-Chinese-American actress known as Awkwafina was born Nora Lum. She said she was quiet, timid, self-conscious, and a passive person growing up. She was bullied a lot as a kid, but her grandmother gave her the courage to embrace all the unique parts of her she wanted to hide earlier in her life.

Awkwafina became her alter-ego personality (nicknamed by a friend). While being Awkwafina, she felt free to be really outspoken, brash, super funny, and a symbol of being who you are.

The biggest take from these examples is... that you are capable of so much greatness if you start to embrace who you are with all your unique talents and strengths. **Being yourself is respecting yourself. There is a mountain of case studies and evidence that shows people are happier if they lean into who they are and appreciate all the things that define themselves: the way they look, the things they like, their quirks, their natural talents, their experiences, and their values.** Harvard Medical School did the longest modern clinical study on happiness. One of the key attributes of happier people was the ability to be themselves.

I also just want to be clear that being you and embracing yourself doesn't mean "I'm fine and I don't need to change". **It doesn't mean you can't improve and become a better version of yourself.** Personal growth is being who you are while evolving as a person. Whenever you get in those down moments when you feel you aren't like everyone else...just remember that can be your strength. **When we embrace our own uniqueness, we let go of the FEAR of not fitting in.**

## SPREADING THE SELF-LOVENESS

True acceptance comes from the inside, and **by accepting ourselves, we often make OTHER people feel comfortable doing the same.** You know what happens when we see someone who is a little different but TOTALLY comfortable and easy in their own skin? They are great to be around! **Don't you feel a sense of openness to do the same and be more comfortable in your own skin?** It's actually inspiring and freeing. Their actions of being who they are give you more freedom to be more of who you are. They are spreading self-love and acceptance around! Yes, it is contagious.

**Accepting your unique self also helps you appreciate differences in other people.** Differences are not limitations but sources of strength and inspiration for the whole group. It would also be too boring and wouldn't make sense if everyone was the same. Being around people different from you opens up your mind and world. It makes you smarter. It also teaches you more compassion and understanding of what it may be like in someone else's shoes.

**One thing to remember is that embracing our uniqueness does not mean isolating ourselves or rejecting the importance of community and the people around us.** It is about truly being ourselves while still valuing and respecting the people around us.

## THE LIGHT TRICK

**TIP:** Here is a quick trick I learned to help me out when I start to feel "not enough". I know there are moments in life where you feel a little out of place and different. This may lead you to feel discouraged or sad. I want you to get into the regular practice of shining your light. Instead of shrinking inward, close your eyes, **picture a small light inside you. Imagine that light getting bigger and bigger and bigger.** You feel a bright light growing inside you. Feel the light shining so big the rays are coming out of you. **Do that for a 30 seconds or a minute. You should start to feel more powerful, calmer and more confident.**

**Do the light trick when you get in the sneaky moments of feeling down, low self-esteem, smaller, afraid. Learn to shine your light bright within you.**

# GROWING YOUR TALENTS AND STRENGTHS

*"See what you are naturally good at and make it part of your routine. That little spark of your natural talent has tremendous power to take you places."*
— *Hiral Nagda*

**You know what really helps boost your confidence and expands your world? Being good at something!**

Every single one of us has natural talents and strengths that we are meant to grow and share. Can you imagine the world without really good movies, amazing musicians who create songs that you love and you connect to, incredible athletes who are so much fun to watch, or even that teacher who is so good at what they do, he/she got you really interested in a subject? Or that person who always makes you feel better because they have a way of saying something that gives you a new perspective. **You have the same magic inside you.** You have special talents, too, and life often gives you signs of what they are.

**Let's dig into YOUR natural talents.** What are your thoughts on what they could be? **Every single one of us is born with some natural talent at something.** This means you are better at some things naturally than other people. Some people can sing and understand music really well. Some can paint and draw so easily, while the rest of us can only draw stick figures;

others are great with numbers or design or anything tech. Some people may have a powerful natural ability for sports. **Even if you haven't found your talent or talents, I promise you, you have them.** You just have to find them.

**They may be talents that you didn't even know were talents.** They are just things that come easily to you. For example, you may be great at being really organized. You may be the person that your friends come to you for advice. **Believe it or not, those are talents too!** Sometimes, our talents are so natural to us that we may take them for granted, assuming everyone has them. However, what comes easily to you may not come that easily for other people.

If you haven't found your natural talent or skill, a sign could be something that lights you up when you are doing it or thinking about it. **Think about what lights you up.** What activities, hobbies, or interests make your heart happy and leave you feeling alive? Take a moment to think about these questions. These answers may have clues to discovering your unique talents and strengths.

**Pay attention to the activities that spark joy within you and bring out your best self.** Consider the skills or hobbies you are good at without trying as hard as everyone else. These could be playing a musical instrument, being a great communicator, problem-solving, or you can easily connect with people or make fast friends. **Start writing this down as the starting point for finding your talents.**

You could also DEVELOP talents through exposure to it, training, and practice. **It just started with some natural ability that you had that eventually grew into a real skill after more training and experience.** For example, say that you like creating things and have a good sense of what goes with what. You think, "This color goes great with that design," etc. **Then, all of a sudden, you get introduced to cooking.** You never really cooked before but after trying it, you find out that you are amazing at putting ingredients together and presenting the dishes beautifully. Who knew this unless you got exposure to it? Then, as you cooked more and more, the more impressive you got at it. And importantly, you love it because it is a creative outlet for you. There are many talents that you have that have yet to be uncovered. **And there is a great sense of confidence and pride when you realize you are good at something right?**

Still trying to figure out what your talents are? **We are now going to talk about something I call the "pull."** What are you naturally drawn to do? What are you "pulled" to do?

For example, everyone has watched a sports game. There are some people who are just driven to practice, analyze, and play every day. They spend all of their spare time focusing on improving. Others may watch a game, just be entertained and that's it. Then they see someone spending so many hours practicing, training, etc., and think, WHY would they put themselves through all that? It's so boring!

Meanwhile, that same person is at the gym every single day, spending hours and hours fine-tuning their game, that they completely lose track of time. Others may spend hours and hours in the art studio covered in paint. Someone else may think singing is the absolute best feeling on earth.

**Sometimes, life can give you signs of what your talents are just by you wanting to do something that other people would never consider doing in their free time**. Again, it is something that lights you up when you see it and do it. Take notice of your pull. Usually, your pull has also something to do with your natural talents. **Growing your natural talents and learning the process is, in itself, a huge life skill.** Noticing and learning your talent will give you more confidence and openness to life experiences. Even if things don't work out exactly the way you had planned, it is great to dabble and check out the pull anyway. Just TRYING something may lead you to something ELSE you are meant or love to do. Be open to the path it takes you on.

One thing is don't use your "pull" as a crutch. **LIFE IS BALANCE.** When you get so focused on your passion, it's so easy to get your life OFF balance. I want to emphasize while it is great to recognize, go with your pull and grow your talents, **do NOT use it as an excuse to neglect other parts of your life**. This is not a calling to neglect your school work or your other responsibilities or to not take good care of yourself. Your pull makes up only part of what you are about.

## STORY OF EMMA WATSON

Emma is most well known for her role in Harry Potter as Hermione Granger. Did you also know she was so shy and had a lot of social anxiety before she was cast in Harry Potter? To help her with her anxiety, she thought it would be a good idea to start acting and felt the "pull" to act. She then discovered she loved it and was great at it. In addition, acting gave her confidence and was an outlet for her creativity while helping her get out of her shell. Today, she is an outspoken, inspirational role model and speaker for people worldwide. This all started with finding her pull.

## STORY OF LIN-MANUEL MIRANDA

He is one of the most famous composers and writers in recent history, creating the breakthrough musical *Hamilton*. When he was younger, he also struggled with social anxiety and shyness. In interviews, he talks about his earlier struggles to fit in. But he discovered his love for writing, performing, and writing rap songs in high school. Music gave him a path to express himself and connect with other people. His "pull" brought out his inner light, creativity, and newfound confidence.

## ARE YOU PULLED BY A PROBLEM?

Some people are naturally drawn to solve a specific problem. That's a natural talent, too. Have you ever seen something or noticed something that someone else wouldn't bother with but for some reason, you are really interested in solving? It could be something you have been thinking about for a while or just came upon by chance.

## STORY OF RYAN HRELJAC

One day, Ryan was sitting in class at an early age and his teacher was discussing how, in parts of the world, some people were sick and even dying because they didn't even have clean water. He learned how, in some parts of Africa, people walked for hours and hours just to get even dirty water. Then he looked at his own life. He could just walk a few feet out of the classroom, go to a drinking fountain, and get clean water. He could walk into the bathroom, turn on a faucet, and wash his hands. He spent gallons every morning showering with clean water.

**He had listened to the same discussion everyone in his class had.** Same words, same teacher. But he was the one who went home that night, and he decided to do something about it. He found his pull...solving a problem that really bothered him. He begged his parents to help him figure out a problem. He promised to do extra chores at home so he could build a well. In his mind, that could help solve the problem. After a couple of months, he earned $70. Then he learned the cost to build a well in Uganda was $2,000, and the problem was much bigger than he realized. When he grew older, he started the Ryan's Well Foundation. He is now a notable speaker on making a difference, no matter who you are or how old you are.

Of course, not every story ends with someone becoming famous or creating a company; often, people can feel out of place in the beginning. But this can be a seed to something else. What I am saying is, that every single person has unique talents that were meant to be his/hers/theirs, AND we are all designed to succeed because all the ingredients are already in there. When you find your talent or talents or pull, growing it can jump-start your confidence journey **simply because being good at something gives you**

**confidence and a sense of purpose.** I also want to remind you that you probably won't be "amazing" at something right away. It all takes a lot of patience, time, hard work, and its own set of challenges.

## STORY OF MICHAEL JORDAN

Everyone knows who Michael Jordan is. It took him a massive amount of time, effort, hard work, and overcoming obstacles to reach his "amazing Mike" peak level. He was cut from his school basketball team when he was a sophomore. But he was drawn to playing, plus he had the physical natural design for the game. He didn't give up and worked on perfecting his skills. He didn't make it to his varsity team until junior year, and that's when more people started to realize his incredible natural talent.

## STRENGTHS

**Let's get to the topic of "strengths".** I group strengths in almost the same group as talents with a twist. Talents are natural abilities you tend to be born with but strengths are natural skills that may draw people to you or a reason people will be drawn to you. Some examples of strengths are empathy, listening skills, leadership, strong intuition, determination, and insightfulness. We all have some natural strengths. You could be the person people go to when they need a pep talk or feel super comfortable talking to. You can be the person who people look toward to take control of a situation and lead on reaching a goal. You can be the person who can stays calm in situations where other people get super stressed out. Or you can be the person who always "gets it done." This comes naturally or easily for you. You may be the person who reaches out more than others when someone is hurting and feels the need to include them.

# ▌WHAT ARE YOUR NATURAL STRENGTHS?

**It is great when you know what your strengths are because when the moment comes when your skills can help, you can step up.** Think about what they are and write them down. You could even ask for some feedback from your friends or family. They may see natural strengths in you that you didn't notice before.

**Here are some examples of strengths:**

**People skills** = Friendly, easy to talk to, great at listening, makes friends easily, enjoys working with others.

**Work ethic** = Hard working and puts in real effort, reliable, doesn't give up easily, gets things done, and sticks to tasks.

**Adaptable** = Can go with the flow, shift when needed, can handle changes without stressing out.

**Great communicator** = Good at expressing yourself, tells stories well, speaks clearly, charismatic, and can keep people engaged when speaking.

**Problem-Solver** = Can figure out solutions to problems, thinks creatively, is resourceful, always looking for ways to fix problems, and analytical.

**Leadership** = Inspires others to take action, takes charge, and gets things going, motivates people, makes decisions when needed (even the tough ones).

**Organizational skills** = Manages time well, can handle multiple things at the same time, gets things done efficiently.

**Positivity** = Keeps a cheerful attitude, looks for the positive in situations, encourages and supports people when they need it, and brings a good vibe to situations.

**Self-motivation**= Stays driven, sets goals and works toward them, takes the initiative on their own to get things done, always looking for ways to improve.

**Integrity** = Honest and truthful, can be trusted, doing what's right (even when no one is watching), reliable, and keeps promises.

**Empathetic**= Understands other people's feelings, cares about what others are going through, shows compassion and kindness, considerate of others' needs.

**Creativity** = Think of things from different angles or different ways, come up with unique ideas, has an imaginative mind, and enjoys expressing in artistic ways.

**Humor** = Witty and funny, enjoys making people laugh and lightens up situations with jokes.

**Calm under pressure** = Stays cool when things get tough, keeps a level head in stressful situations and can think clearly, doesn't easily get freaked out.

**Tech savvy** = Comfortable with technology, quick to learn new apps and anything tech.

**What strengths do you think you have?**

_____

_____

_____

_____

## DEVELOPING YOUR NATURAL TALENTS AND STRENGTHS

**Now that you have found some of your talents and strengths, you need to find time to nurture and develop them.** Just like a seed needs care and environment to grow into a thriving tree, your talents need attention and practice to reach their potential if that is what you want. Practice and give yourself room and opportunities to grow your talents. Take classes, read books, go to workshops, and watch videos on how to improve. Find people experienced in your talent you can talk to for guidance and inspire you to improve. Ask them what it was like on their journey. **You can learn so much by just talking to people who have been through what you are about to go through.** You learn shortcuts, how to avoid mistakes that they went through, and what it took to go from here to there.

Build a support system of people who can help your vibe and help your talent and strengths grow. It helps to be around people who share your interests and passions. They can provide great feedback, keep you going when you get sidetracked, and challenge and inspire you along the way. Welcome feedback, both positive and constructive, for it is through this type of back and forth that you can improve.

## ▌ DON'T BE AFRAID TO FAIL

"The secret of life is to fail seven times and to get up eight times."
— *Paulo Coelho*

**Understand getting really good at something takes time... literally for everyone.** It goes from just starting, to getting OK, to getting better, to getting great... it takes a lot of persistence, patience, and constant learning. A VERY important thing to remember: **DON'T BE AFRAID TO FAIL.** Most people who are amazing at what they do **only got there because they failed more times than most other people**. Failure is not failure but really a chance to grow, see where you went wrong, and learn from mistakes. **Failure is a stepping stone toward success.** Give yourself the freedom to fail. Allow yourself room to experiment, fall down, take some risks, and learn from both wins and setbacks.

**Remember that growth doesn't always go in a straight line.** There will be times when your growth may be slower than you want. Don't let these times discourage you. There are days you won't be as good as you think you can be. There are days you will be tired, cranky, distracted, have a lot on your plate, or just sheer bad luck. **Understand the process and be patient with yourself.** Celebrate even the smallest wins, for they are markers of your growth and progress. Forgive yourself for your mistakes. Know it's OK to make mistakes because you know, with confidence, you can do better.

**Think of a time when you failed but got right back up and succeeded (it could be even after numerous failures)**

_____

_____

_____

_____

_____

**What made you pick yourself up after you failed?**

_____

_____

_____

**How did you feel after you succeeded?**

_____

_____

**Write about an accomplishment that you are the proudest about.**

_____

_____

_____

_____

_____

_____

## TIP: PICTURE THE FEELING: TAKE MENTAL SNAPSHOT

When there is something that you want to accomplish or succeed at I want you to close your eyes and take a mental snapshot of that moment of accomplishing your "proudest" thing. I want you to remember that feeling you had vividly and feel it in your body. Then, I want you to bring that same feeling to whatever you want to accomplish. **See yourself succeeding and bring that same feeling to the event in your head.**

## BE CURIOUS AND EXPLORE

Even though it feels great to focus on your existing talents, do not be afraid to explore new areas. **Sometimes, your true passion and love are in areas you haven't experienced yet.** Sometimes, your potential lies beyond the boundaries of what you initially think you are capable of. Be open to opportunities to step outside your comfort zone and try new things related to your talents. **Curiosity and stepping out of what you are normally used to, or even doing things you don't think you can do, are powerful ways to grow and learn more about yourself.**

Let yourself be curious about other areas or interests that align with your talents and even some that don't. And don't worry about looking like you don't know something or being bad in the beginning. Everyone started as a beginner. **No one was born being absolutely perfect and amazing in their talent.** All you need is the willingness to grow and learn. Being curious and trying new things will help you see things a bit differently and even uncover hidden talents you never knew you had!

It is also actually really cool when you can blend different talents and skills you have learned into something new.

**Write down some things you are curious about. It could be anything you want to explore, like places, activities, food... whatever comes to mind.**

_____

_____

_____

_____

_____

_____

## SHARING YOUR TALENTS WITH THE WORLD

One of the best things about having talents and skills is that you can share them with the world. Growing your talents is not just for you. Your unique gifts are meant to be shared with the world, impacting the lives of others and creating a ripple effect of impact, benefits, and a positive vibe.

Remember the purpose of growing your talents is not solely about recognition or success. **It is about who you truly are inside and letting your**

**light shine.** Follow your passions, nurture your abilities, and let your talents shine brightly for the rest of the world to see.

Just think of all the ways your talents can make a difference. You could inspire, lead, uplift, and entertain in so many small and big ways. Whether through creating art, helping people feel better, solving problems, making people laugh, entertaining, or inspiring. Yes, your talents can help people in ways that you may not even have realized. You have the ability to be really impactful.

**What are some ways you think your strengths and talents can benefit the people around you and the world?**

_____

_____

_____

_____

_____

_____

*Chapter Four*

# THE COMPARISON TRAP, AND NON-TOXIC SOCIAL MEDIA SURFING

## THE OTHER TYPE OF PEER PRESSURE

Now that we have gone through some of the things that can bring us up... let's explore some things that can take us down—chronically comparing yourself to others. So, let's start with the most obvious comparison trap: social media...**the different type of peer pressure.** It's supposed to be entertainment, right? Yes, we can learn some things from social media, but its main purpose is entertainment via getting the MOST eyeballs. In the short 5 minutes of passing time through class, you are tapping, saving, and liking, **but it's the peer pressure that doesn't seem like peer pressure.**

It's not other people pushing you to act, look, and think a certain way. **It's peer pressure in the way it makes you feel about yourself and your life in a way that you can't help but compare with others.** But the reality is that for every person someone is liking and seeing on Instagram, TikTok, Snapchat, **there are far more sitting at home watching TV doing nothing or at school or work trying to pass the time.**

So, while during the teen years, you are trying to find out who you are, you are also seeing an alternate version of life that simply isn't real over and over again every single day. **The standards put out on social media are simply not attainable for anyone... not even for the people posting their fabulous lives.** They are not being real. But you get mentally pushed to do something, be someone, act like someone because you think everyone else is doing that, and you sometimes feel left out or not enough. **How often have you scrolled through social media and felt terrible about yourself?** How many times a day?

## BUILD YOUR CONFIDENCE ABOUT WHAT YOU THINK OF YOURSELF (NOT OTHERS)

"**You are giving your personal power away every time you seek validation from only outside of yourself.**"
— *Nadia Walker*

I want to give you one of the biggest secrets of a happier life. **Never build your self-confidence MAINLY around what other people are thinking about you.** Because that only means YOUR self-confidence will go up or down based on how/what THEY think of you (which changes ALL the time, and you don't have control over). This never allows you to be who you really are and meant to be.

**Write about a time when you think you worried too much about what other people were thinking... that you ended up not doing what was right for you?**

_____

_____

_____

_____

_____

_____

Your self-confidence has to come from the inside. Stop chasing happiness based on what others think of you. It never ever lasts and keeps the best version of you from coming out. So, find your self-confidence by finding out who you are, embracing who you are, and striving to be the best version of yourself.

**Another problem with self-confidence built solely around what people think of you is that they are not playing YOUR game.** What I mean by that is, say you are LeBron James, and you are on the court. There are thousands of people shouting things at you, good and bad. Do you think he stops the game and listens to what they are saying? NOPE. He is the one playing the game, he is the one practicing every day, he is the one putting in the time, this is his career. **This is his game. Those people are just shouting from the BLEACHERS. It's not their game. It's HIS game. Remember, your life is YOUR game.** Of course, you want to be open to hearing other people's opinions and thoughts of those you trust. You need feedback and conversation, advice from others. You are part of a larger community and it's better to hear people out. **Just knowing how YOU feel about yourself is the most important thing.**

## ▌PEOPLE DON'T THINK ABOUT YOU AS MUCH AS YOU THINK THEY DO

**Another secret I want to let you in on is that most people don't think about you all that much (or at least as much as you think).** Most people are caught up in themselves, their own lives, their own thoughts and drama. They aren't thinking all day about how you fell in front of everyone at school, if you screwed up your presentation in front of everyone, your shirt with a stain on it, that zit on your face or all the other things you think people care about. The fact is, they don't really. Maybe it's registering in their brains as a mini bleep thought at most (probably not even), but that's it. You know why? And this isn't supposed to come off as people being selfish or that you don't matter. **The reality is, most people's priorities are themselves, not**

**you.** So stop worrying so much about what other people think of you... they aren't. **They are thinking more about themselves.**

## ▌BUILDING A HEALTHY RELATIONSHIP WITH SOCIAL MEDIA

So, what happens when you start to feel bad about yourself scrolling through social media? **Building a good relationship with social media means knowing when to pull it back. Pay attention to how much you're using it and HOW IT IS AFFECTING YOUR MOOD AND MENTAL STATE.** Take breaks when needed and prioritize real-life connections and experiences OVER what's happening online. **When you get in those moments when you think social media is affecting your self-worth and creating an unhealthy view of yourself, first, step back.** Take as much time as you need to regain better perspective. "Feel" the amount of time that is right for you. It could be days or weeks, but whatever you need to get back to "balance". **Don't feel pressured to see everything that is going on, and let FOMO (fear of missing out) creep in.** Your mindset is much more important.

**Write about a time when scrolling through social media got you really down because you were comparing your life to someone else's?**

_____

_____

_____

_____

_____

**Secondly, notice what specifically is triggering those feelings.** During your break, think of ways to deal with those specific triggers. For example, if they are body image issues, then remind yourself (even keep journals around to write out) that the lives on social media are not as real as people are posting. They ONLY post (almost always with a filter) what THEY want you to see, not their real life. Secondly, write out the positives about yourself. Remember, you are meant to live YOUR life and not anyone else's. Remember, **social media should enhance your life, not consume it or determine your self-worth.**

**Write about some trigger events from social media you notice that kick off some feelings of low self-worth.**

_____

_____

_____

_____

_____

**Can you identify what those feelings are?**

_____

_____

_____

_____

**Write some things you love about yourself (write as many as you can)**

_____

_____

_____

_____

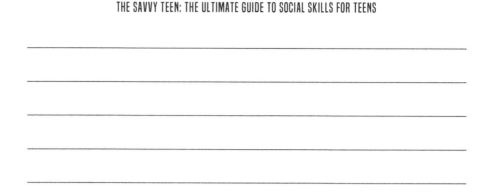

When you are posting your own life don't forget you can control your story and decide your value. If you want to use social media in a healthy way, you've got to work on having a positive mindset. **Be proud of what makes you different and take time to notice and celebrate your own wins. Instead of trying to fit in with what everyone else is doing, focus on growing as a person and what fills up your spirit.** When you do this, you'll start a journey of getting to know yourself better and being true to who you are, which will help you handle social media with confidence and strength.

## MAKING COMPARISONS IN THE REAL WORLD

This goes for comparing yourself to people around you in real life. **When you start to feel bad because you are comparing yourself to others, take a step back.** Remember all the unique and positive traits, talents, and skills about yourself. Also, don't beat yourself up if you do make comparisons sometimes. If you do, recognize it and then let it go.

## OUR BRAINS ARE HARD-WIRED TO COMPARE TO SURVIVE

I also want you to know that comparisons, labeling, etc., are actually hard-wired in our brains naturally, so it is very human to do this. Just recognize when it becomes toxic.

Let me explain why we naturally compare anyway. It all has to do with how our brain works when we are just trying to survive. The human brain automatically compares everything. This vs that. **It's a survival trait.**

Our brain naturally collects comparison information to reduce the "unknown." Our brains get bombarded and slammed with so much info all the time that comparing and labeling help us to SIMPLIFY mass amounts of information coming at us every single day. **What I am saying is that our brain NATURALLY compares things all the time**, including me vs other people type of information, **to process things SIMPLER AND FASTER.** Otherwise, our brains would go on complete overload.

If our brains didn't compare and label things fast, we would have too many "unknowns" or not know what things mean to us. **Our brains DO NOT like unknowns**. WHY do our brains not like unknowns? **We instinctively view unknowns as a threat or something that would possibly hurt us.** This goes way back to our caveman days of survival. Back in primitive times, to survive, man had to figure out quickly what was harmful or harmless to avoid danger. We had to label, compare, and categorize.

Now, in modern times, we still have this instinct of comparing, labeling, and categorizing everything super fast. **Basically, the more we know what something IS vs something else, the SAFER we naturally feel.** That's why it's a survival trait. But it gets toxic and unhealthy if all your actions, views, and feelings are based on you constantly comparing yourself to other people.

**In addition, our brains instinctively believe it's safer to be part of a group.** In caveman times, it WAS safer to be part of a community for survival. We feel safer " fitting in".

**So those natural tendencies of needing "to fit in" and "comparing" go back a really long time and were needed to live day to day.** Still, in modern times, when we are less likely to be hurt by things around us, we have to watch out when those hard-wired tendencies emotionally weigh us down.

When you are "fitting in," remember to fit in with the right community. Your "people" should support, encourage, and accept who you are. **Connect** with people who appreciate and uplift you rather than be around people who have toxic standards or conversations.

Write down some people who uplift you (that you know and don't know). This could be people around you or even people that you haven't met. For example, I loved music growing up, and some songs and artists just lifted me up when I listened to them.

_____

_____

_____

_____

_____

_____

_____

# Chapter Five

# OVERCOMING ANXIETY, FEAR
# (AND OTHER EMOTIONAL MONSTERS)

We ALL have fear, anxiety, depression, guilt, shame, and embarrassment at times. Even the coolest person you can think of has been through it. Famous people, your teachers, your parents, the cute person you crush on... literally everyone has felt these emotions at some point in their life and had to get through it. During the teen years, with all the changes going on, these emotions can get really, really big. I am going to give you some helpful hacks on tackling these emotions so you can feel better equipped to handle them as they come up.

I will tackle two of the biggest monsters first, but let's get something straight and clear before that. The most important thing I want you to remember is that sometimes, people may not completely OVERCOME anxiety, fear, and other emotional monsters, as if those feelings completely disappear. **Those feelings can still pop up, but you can learn how not to let them take the wheel.** They may still exist, BUT we can learn how to move through them to the back of the bus. And when those big feelings try to TAKE the wheel again, take it right back. So, these emotions may come along for the ride, but they take the back seat. **And then, over time, those "monster" feelings take the farthest seat back.** So when you see some people being "brave" it's not so much that they have zero fear or anxiety. They have anxiety and fear just like you do, just like the rest of us. **They just take those emotions along with them for the ride (shove them to the back of the bus), keep moving** forward through life, and do what they have to do. You can do the same thing!

# ANXIETY

Let's start with anxiety. What does anxiety feel like? **It feels like a moment, or event has completely hijacked your brain, and you freeze.** Picture this. You have to give a speech in front of class. You start to get a panic attack. You think, "I'm going to stutter. I hate all these people looking at me. I just want to be somewhere else. I can't take all this attention on me. I'm going to mess up." All you think of is failure, screwing up, and then you look terrified on top of it. Your heart is racing out of your chest. You start shaking. "What is happening here? I didn't realize I was going to feel THIS panicked. I'm being stupid about this. What is wrong with me? I have to do great on this speech because it's 30% of my final grade!".

**Write about a time when your body just froze from anxiety or fear.**

_____

_____

_____

_____

_____

**What were some of the thoughts you had going through your head during that time?**

_____

_____

_____

_____

# FIGHT OR FLIGHT

**What is happening in your body is something called the FIGHT OR FLIGHT response.** What is it? Why do we have it? Fight or flight response is an automatic physical reaction to an event that we THINK is frightening or very stressful and harmful. When this response kicks in, your heart starts to race. Certain chemicals in the brain PREPARE the body to be active **(getting ready to stay, fight, or run)**. Palms can get sweaty, your body shakes, and oxygen flows to your muscles. **The response can be triggered by both real and imaginary thoughts.**

**We have it from way back (from caveman days again) as a survival mechanism.** Back when we were cavemen, we NEEDED this response because there were real physical dangers around, and your body needed an internal alert system for danger. In other words, our bodies needed to get ready to literally fight (get active) or escape (take flight or run) when we sensed danger, harm, or a stressful situation like getting chased by a dinosaur. We STILL have the automatic human response when we sense something scary in our brain! That's your body's natural fight or flight response kicking in. All the blood flows to your heart and muscles, getting ready to be active. **But standing in front of the classroom, you can't fight. Your body wants to run (or flight), but you can't go anywhere.** So your body ends up feeling like it's freaking out. **What can you do to get out of it?**

**There are three parts to anxiety.** When an event or threatening thought kicks it off, **A:** Our beliefs (what we say to ourselves) then **B:** the physical happens (how our body reacts), then **C:** our behaviors or what we want to do (running or getting out of the situation).

**The event :** I am giving my speech and doing terribly. **Belief** = My class thinks I'm stupid. **Body reacting** = Brain freezing, body sweating, heart pounding, I can't speak clearly. **Behavior** = Wanting to run out of class (or actually doing it).

## ▌ SOLUTIONS

**First: BECOME THE WATCHER.** Not only can this help with anxiety, but many other internal "monsters." **Understand you are NOT your emotions. You are just someone who is FEELING or having those emotions.** There is a BIG difference. For example, instead of saying, "I am scared, I am nervous". **You are someone who is feeling nervous or feeling scared and having those emotions but NOT the actual emotion. That means you can watch these emotions from an outside observer's perspective.** WATCH your emotions rather than BE your emotions. For example, notice when you are feeling something and then realize," I am feeling this or that," like you have stepped away and are watching your emotions.

Think of it like someone watching a play or a game. You are watching someone catch the ball but not in it. You are only WATCHING what's happening. Get it? **You AREN'T your thoughts, but you are just watching your thoughts as they go in and out of your head. This step helps you get out of the drama of the event.** It helps give you a different view of your emotions and helps reduce stress. Be the watcher instead. Just step back and watch. This will help with all types of feelings like anger, jealousy, guilt, and shame. **It will help you think of emotions as THERE, and you are HERE, like watching a movie.**

**Second: BREATHE.** Take a really deep breath in and slowly exhale like you are exhaling the emotions out. Do this 5-10 times. Count on your fingers 1,2,3, etc., if that helps. **As you start paying more attention to your breath, you should begin to feel less anxious. Your mind has a hard time focusing on more than one big task.** Give it something else to focus on.

Third: <u>CHANGE YOUR WORDS. CHANGE YOUR THOUGHTS</u>. **Listen to what you are telling yourself.** For example, are you saying, "I'm going to completely screw up," or "I can't do this". Turn it right around and think, "I got this," "I can do this," "Everything is going to be ok".

**Say it again and again. What you tell yourself is the most important conversation you will have. Be supportive of yourself.**

Go back to the scenario you wrote about above. How could you have changed your thoughts to be more supportive of yourself?

_____

_____

_____

_____

_____

Fourth: **<u>TAKE A MOMENT</u>. The reality is there are times in life when you are just too overwhelmed.** And no amount of THINKING can get you out of it. For example, you have five things all happening at the same time, or you have five things you have to do at the same time. You become so overwhelmed that you are frozen and can't move at all. You just don't know what to do. A big wave of panic comes over you. Observing, breathing, and changing your thoughts are not helping as much as expected. It's just too hard to handle. **The best thing to do is to take 5-10 minutes (maybe longer/less) and do ABSOLUTELY NOTHING for a bit.** Let your brain and body reset. **Just sit and do nothing,** just **like a computer. Stop, shut down, take a minute and restart.** Then get back into it.

# ▌FEAR

Anxiety and fear are buddies. They go hand in hand, as when there is one, the other is around somewhere. Fear is your brain naturally interpreting something as a threat to your mind to your emotional or physical well-being. Your heart starts to race (because your body wants to be alert and is getting ready to protect itself). Whether the threat is real or imaginary, your body reacts the same.

When you start to get the feeling of your body/brain getting super jumpy because it is trying to warn you of something harmful coming...break down where the fear is coming from and if it's legit. **Basically, is it rational, or is it irrational?**

**Fear is useful in a sense because it does actually try to protect us.** If you are trying to cross a really busy intersection and there are a ton of cars coming, then you should have some rational fear that gives your body the signal to keep an eye out and be very careful when crossing. This fear prompts you to be more cautious when you should be.

On the other hand, say you absolutely REFUSE to go into the water anywhere because you are afraid of sharks. You won't go into lakes, streams, warm beach water, or even a pool. **This is an irrational fear.** They will not be sharks in a freshwater lake. There won't be sharks in a stream. But you still have this fear, even knowing it doesn't make sense. **For a lot of adults, if they don't address their fears, these irrational emotions can stay with them into adulthood.**

**First, address where this fear is coming from.** Did you happen to spend hours watching "Shark Week" as a kid, and now you are deathly afraid of sharks? Did you watch *Jaws*, and you got completely freaked out? **Sometimes, you may not even know where the fear started from, and that's OK.**

**Second,** even though it may be really tough, start a game plan to face this fear head-on. You know what you do? **Rewire your brain and change the association**. Change the immediate association of an action from something harmful to something that is not so bad or even fun. You have to put yourself in the situation of facing your fear over and over again. **When nothing harmful happens to you, your body will start associating the action that triggered the fear, like swimming in a lake or going into the water, with something that is NO LONGER a threat.** You may still have a hint of that fear in the back of your mind, but it no longer hijacks your brain.

> **"The way to gain confidence is to do what you are afraid to do."**
> — *Swati Sharma*

This is exactly what happened to my daughter. She had a real terror of sharks. She didn't like to go into any water where she couldn't see clearly to the bottom or if there were any creatures in the water. Even if they were cute little helpful fish. She refused to go kayaking, swimming, or even on boats.

One day, we decided it was time she sent this fear to the back of the bus. She was missing out on so many amazing experiences in the water with family and friends because of her fear. Not only that, she was missing out on the experience of seeing incredible sea life, the beautiful ocean or lake environment, and broadening her world.

PLUS, I wanted her to go through the entire experience of having an immobilizing fear and learn the skills of facing and overcoming it. **You see, this won't be the last fear she has in her life.** As she gets older, there will be many things that she may have an irrational fear about.

But she will have learned how to overcome them step by step, by being patient and loving with herself, and seeing the amazing results of doing something she had initially feared. **There are incredible experiences, people, and benefits on the OTHER side of fear. She ALSO will get a**

**massive confidence boost by doing something she didn't think she could do.**

So that day, we put her in the kayak. She initially got really nervous and kind of freaked out, but we all decided to be patient with her fear. We all were right around her and always in eye view if she felt nervous or threatened. We told her it would be OK and just to get through it. **The VERY first step is to just get through it.** Again, brave people still have fear, but they don't let it take the wheel. She was very courageous that day.

She went kayaking that day with all of us. She didn't love that she was still afraid but got through it.

Then the next day we went into the ocean. Again, her fear propped up. But slowly, she went in step by step. We put her in the water numerous times, each time addressing her fear, and each time, it got better and better. **Her mind and her body were no longer threatened by the action of going into the water just by repetition.**

Today, not only does she have zero problems getting in the water, but she LOVES trying new experiences and challenges even though she may initially be afraid. WHY? **Because she learned the useful life skill of not letting your fears take the wheel and driving the emotional bus.** Yes, that's right, she moved that fear right to the back. Don't get me wrong, she still doesn't like sharks, and the fear is still in the back of her head, BUT her fear is no longer irrational.

She just ran her very first half marathon and finished second in her age group. She is rising up, facing challenges, and looking for new areas of growth. Now, **when she comes across something that can be a bit scary or out of her comfort zone, she has the confidence to go for it and see where it leads her.** Because of her love of seeking new challenges, she found another passion of hers...running races.

When an irrational fear comes up, it can also be turned into a signal that something new and interesting is around the corner.

Think of some fears that you may have and write them down.

_____

_____

_____

_____

**Think of a fear you REALLY want to overcome.** For example, if you fear spiders, I'm not sure your life would be all that changed if you addressed that fear. **Think of a fear that may be blocking you from experiencing life to the fullest.**

_____

_____

_____

_____

Now think what your life would be like in terms of the benefits to your life if you faced your fears and kicked them to the back of the bus.

_____

_____

_____

_____

_____

If you really want to face your fear, think of some things you can do to get past it. You can also recruit people you trust to help you and be there for you, like your family, close friends, or mentors.

_____

_____

_____

_____

_____

**Facing your fears socially is really useful for your life, too.** For example, do you know the number one thing most people are THE MOST terrified of? It's not sharks, it's not planes, it's heights, and it is not even death. **It is speaking in front of a large audience.** Yup. Making a fool of yourself giving a speech in front of a live audience was voted the number one worst nightmare for many people. So basically, social fear feels just as threatening to your brain as physical fear.

So, I think you know what I am going to say. The BEST way to overcome something like this is to join a debate club, volunteer first to get your presentation in front of class, etc.

One thing I want to acknowledge is that, especially **in the beginning, things may or may not go smoothly when you face your fears, but that's OK.** Pick yourself up and move on because it is all part of the learning process. Yes, you may fumble the ball, but so does everyone sometimes. You will get through it, and it will be fine.

Now that you are armed with facing what is perceived as the number one fear of most people, think of how much more confident you will be when you have to go up and start a conversation with someone new, lead a group, or walk into a new situation. You are building up your confidence toolbox to handle whatever comes at you.

## GUILT AND SHAME

We all walk through life carrying big and little guilts and shames packed inside of us. This is completely normal. **Sometimes, a little guilt is just common sense.** We should feel a bit guilty for being mean to someone, not telling the truth when we should have, or not taking responsibility for our actions. Just like a little bit of fear is good to keep us safe, a little guilt is good to keep our actions and words in check.

What isn't healthy is when this guilt and shame start to take us down a rabbit hole of low self-esteem, internal bashing, and low self-worth. **When that happens, you need to kick them to the back of the bus, too.**

## REMIND YOURSELF IT'S OK BUT OWN UP

We all go through life making big and little mistakes. **Understand everyone does the best with what they know at that time.** You may think," if I had known this and that, I would have never done what I did or said what I did". Maybe you were just going through a stressful time. **Don't let that moment DEFINE you.** Mistakes happen and know that you are not alone so stop beating yourself up.

> **"You can learn great things from your mistakes when you aren't busy denying them."**
> — *Stephen R. Covey*

**Understanding we are human and can make mistakes doesn't give a green light to pretend mistakes didn't happen.** If you act like you didn't make a mistake and don't own up to it, then you are not being honest with yourself and are not opening the door to improvement. Even worse, if your actions affect other people, they could be upset and hurt. Denial of responsibility is not remorseful or apologetic for the impact you caused. Take responsibility for your mistakes. **Sometimes, the actual denial of responsibility is MORE upsetting than the mistake itself.** Very few things are more irritating to people than someone who doesn't own up to what he/she/they did and own up correctly. What I mean by correctly is sincerely...not because they were forced to or reluctantly, but because they really deep down are sorry.

## FIGURE OUT WHAT WENT DOWN

Reflect on the situation. If there is a way to make things right, step up and go for it. Apologize if needed or take steps to fix what you can.

Sometimes, you may feel guilty about something that happened that wasn't even in your control. Always remember, **no ONE moment in life defines who you are.** Learn what you can from it and bounce back. You are the one in control of your life narrative. Take that power back.

**Write down some things you feel guilty about that you finally want to let go of? Go ahead...set them free.**

_____

_____

_____

_____

_____

_____

# ▌THE INTERNAL VIOLET FLAME TRICK

When we have thoughts of guilt, shame, embarrassment, and other negative thoughts and feelings that break down our self-worth, I use a little imagery technique. **When those sneaky thoughts and emotions pop up, I think of an internal purple flame, and I send the thoughts and feelings right into the flame, burn it, and envision it disappearing.** I see the thought turn into smoke and dissolve in my mind. If I need to, I do it over and over again.

As silly as it may sound, we often do the opposite. **We accumulate "dust bunnies" of negative thoughts and feelings without even realizing it.** We have one negative thought that leads to more self-bashing negative thoughts, and they keep sprouting more until we have a big cloud of mass negative thoughts that feed each other floating around in our head because we didn't stop them at the start.

When something pops up that isn't supportive of you as a person, send that thought to the purple flame. Stop it right at the beginning.

**Write some other internal thoughts you want to send to the violet flame.**

_____

_____

_____

_____

_____

**Now close your eyes and envision them being burned by the candle and disappearing.**

# CHAT IT OUT

If the guilt and shame or other emotions become too much for you to handle, find someone you trust, like a family member, coach, mentor, or wise friend, and talk through it. Everyone has been through similar stuff, and they can give you some guidance.

# GET TO KNOW AND UNDERSTAND YOUR EMOTIONAL MONSTERS BETTER

**Spot Your Triggers**: Figure out what makes these emotional monsters wake up and kick start. Maybe keep a regular journal to jot down when those anxious thoughts pop up and what's happening around you. You'll see patterns and clues to what's causing the stress.

**Think of some triggers for these emotional monsters. What specifically is happening to cause these emotions to come out? Write them out:**

_____

_____

_____

_____

_____

_____

**Be Kind to Yourself**: When anxiety or other overwhelming feelings come knocking, treat yourself like you'd treat a close friend you care about who is in a tough spot. Be nice and remember that these emotions are totally normal responses to stress or other events that may be happening in your life. **Instead of beating yourself up, give yourself a pep talk and some love.**

<u>Call Out the Crazy Thoughts</u>: **Overwhelming emotions love to mess with your head and create thoughts that don't make sense.** Question those thoughts and look for evidence that proves them wrong. Find more balanced ways to see things and stop the negative chatter.

For example, you made a mistake, or you think you looked terrible one day or did badly on a test. If you have a thought, "I am so ugly", "I am so stupid", "I am the worst! Why can't I get anything right?" **I call these "drama queen" thoughts. They are blowing things way out of proportion and are just around to make you feel extra bad about yourself.** And when you get a bunch of "drama queens" together, they can cause some damage. See them for what they are. Useless gossip that is completely wrong or trying to make something tiny into something huge because they have nothing else better to do.

Put the "drama queen" thoughts in their place. Talk to them like you are defending your best friend when they are bad-mouthing your bestie on fake talk, just trying to him/her/them feel terrible about themselves.

**Think of some "drama queen" thoughts you recently had that know you aren't true.**

_____

_____

_____

_____

**Now flip those thoughts around and turn them into supportive thoughts that you would tell your best friend.**

_____

**Be OK with Uncertainty**: Anxiety and fear hate it when you're cool with not knowing everything. Life is full of surprises, so try not to control or predict every little thing. Accepting uncertainty will help relieve a lot of stress in your life. Embrace the mystery and trust that you can handle whatever comes your way. **There is no way in life you can control everything because you aren't meant to. None of us are smart enough to see the total "good" in some "bad" situations and the "good" from "bad" situations.**

**Call up your emotional wizards**: Sometimes, you might need to call in a trained pro. Therapists or counselors are like emotional wizards. They can help you figure out what's really going on and give you personalized tips to tackle it face to face.

**Remember, beating these emotional monsters is a journey that takes time**. Be patient with yourself and celebrate every little win along the way. With these tricks, you'll build up your strength, learn how to handle tough moments, and kick the monsters to the curb. You've got this.

# *Chapter Six*
## SETTING HEALTHY BOUNDARIES AND TAKING CARE OF YOU

This chapter is about making sure you've got boundaries that keep you feeling good about yourself and your relationships. We'll get into how to figure out what you're OK with (and what's a no-go) and how to talk about your boundaries in a way that's respectful. **It's on YOU to set and stick to your own healthy boundaries** to boost your confidence and well-being. Don't let anyone pressure you into something that just doesn't feel right to you deep down. Listen to that inner voice that says doing something mean, harmful, or toxic just because everyone else is doing it, isn't cool. Trust your gut when it's telling you it's not the right move for you.

## ▌WHAT EXACTLY ARE BOUNDARIES?

It's super important to have boundaries to stay healthy and keep growing as a person. Boundaries are limits established to protect yourself from being hurt, manipulated, or taken advantage of. **In other words, boundaries are your personal limits that you set to make sure nobody messes with you, uses you, or hurts you.** They show others how much you value yourself, what you stand for, who you are, and how you expect to be treated. Boundaries let others know what you tolerate. **It is an extension of self-worth and self-esteem.** In fact, I found that people who have healthy boundaries tend to be the most selfless people. **Healthy boundaries are part of successful friendships and relationships all around.** In order to establish healthy boundaries, you MUST be able to recognize how you feel, what your limits are and to communicate this clearly and honestly.

## FINDING OUT YOUR BOUNDARIES

If you want to have good boundaries, the first step is figuring out what you're cool with and what's just a no-go. **Start by keeping an eye on your emotions and what's going on in your body.** Pay attention when you start feeling uncomfortable, annoyed, or like someone's getting all up in your personal space. **These are probably signs that your boundaries may need to be looked after.** Take some time to think about what really matters to you, what you need, and what you like. Listen to that little voice inside when it's saying something's just not right for you.

## SPOTTING STUFF THAT'S NOT OK

To make sure your boundaries are working for you, you've got to know when someone's doing stuff that's just not cool. While what's unacceptable can vary from person to person, some things are usually a no-go. **This can be things like trying to manipulate you, always putting you down, not respecting your space, any kind of abuse, or just plain lying.** When you can recognize these behaviors and see how they're messing with your well-being, you can step up and protect yourself from them.

## TRUST YOUR GUT

**Your gut feeling is like your secret weapon for having good boundaries.** Sometimes, when something's off, you just get this weird feeling like things aren't quite right. Pay attention to those feelings because they're like your body's way of warning you about stuff that could be bad for you. Take a moment to notice and really listen to that inner voice of yours, and give it some respect. If something feels off, it's a sign that your boundaries might be getting pushed too far. **Again, you will see a theme of identifying your feelings as key to so many things, right?**

There will be times when you find yourself in difficult situations with friends or dating, where you may struggle to communicate your values and what is comfortable for you. There are times when your gut is going to be giving you nudges that someone is crossing a line. You have to figure out how to articulate that you are uncomfortable with a situation. This is essential in all relationships. Remember, boundaries are not selfish or being a prude. **They are necessary for your overall physical, emotional, and mental well-being.**

For example, say you are out with your friends, and they are all drinking heavily. They think it's fun and cool, but in your opinion, they are just going overboard. They keep pressuring you to join in, "You have no idea what you are missing," or "It's not a big deal; just do it." You don't want to come across as "not fun," but you don't feel right about it. But it doesn't matter if it is a big deal or a little deal. **If it doesn't feel right to you and your inner alarm goes off, generally, it isn't for you.**

**Write about a scenario where you felt your boundaries were being pushed or violated.**

_____

_____

_____

_____

_____

**Remember when I said you should go to your gut and use your values as guardrails?** If something doesn't feel right to you, then it doesn't matter what anyone else thinks. Most importantly, it's about what YOU think and feel. If you feel like your boundaries are being overstepped because someone/people are pressuring you into something that doesn't feel right to you. **Learn to say no with calm confidence. Go back to your value system on "self-respect."** Don't worry about FOMO (fear of missing out). **Trust**

me, there will be PLENTY of new opportunities for you to have fun or do something that you will FEEL GOOD about in the future. Don't do things you don't feel right about just to impress/please other people.

**What values you think they violated in the above scenario you wrote about?**

_____

_____

_____

_____

**Looking back now is there anything you would have done differently? And why?**

_____

_____

_____

_____

_____

**Here are some examples of unhealthy and healthy boundaries:**

**Personal Space:**

- **Unhealthy:** Always expecting your someone to hang out with you and getting upset when they spend time with others.
- **Healthy:** Giving someone space to spend time with other people and understanding that everyone needs time alone.

*Example of how to explain your boundaries to someone:* "I need some alone time after school to recharge. It's nothing personal; I just value my space. Hope you understand!"

**Communication:**

- **Unhealthy:** Bombarding someone with messages and getting upset if they don't respond immediately.
- **Healthy**: Understanding that people have different communication styles and giving them the space to reply when they can.

*Example of how to explain your boundaries to someone:* "I sometimes can't pick up the phone so I prefer texting over phone calls for now. Can we communicate that way most of the time?"

**Time Management:**

- **Unhealthy:** Expecting someone to drop everything and help you whenever you want.
- **Healthy:** Understanding that everyone has responsibilities and commitments and respecting their time.

*Example of how to explain your boundaries to someone:* "I know sometimes plans change last minute but I can't always drop everything to hang out. Let's try to make plans in advance so I can manage my time better."

**Privacy Boundaries:**

- **Unhealthy:** Ignoring your friend's request to not share certain personal information and babbling to other people about his/her/their private business.
- **Healthy**: Being mindful of your friend's boundaries and not sharing information that they've asked to keep private.

*Example of how to explain your boundaries to someone:* "I don't feel comfortable with other people knowing about this, even if we're close. Please respect and understand my wishes to keep this private."

**Peer Pressure:**

- **Unhealthy:** Trying to convince someone through guilt, embarrassment or manipulation to do something they are uncomfortable with even though that person realizes it isn't right for them.

- **Healthy:** Respecting someone's decision not to participate in something that they feel isn't right for them.

*Example of how to explain your boundaries to someone:* "I've decided not to drink. I hope you respect my decision and don't pressure me."

## TELLING OTHERS ABOUT YOUR BOUNDARIES NICELY

Once you know your boundaries, it's really important to let other people know about them in a way that's clear but also respectful. Just say what you're cool with and what you're not. Also, try using "I" statements so you're not blaming or coming off as all confrontational.

The "I" statement focuses more on how YOU are feeling versus the "you" statement. For example, saying," I felt hurt when I heard you told this person about my family because it made me think my privacy wasn't respected". Instead of "You didn't listen and don't care about my feelings or respect me ". **You hear the tone?** There is a focus on how it made you feel, and the other statement just sounded like blame. We will delve further into "tone" in another chapter.

**It's also good to practice being assertive and saying "no" when necessary.** Remember, setting boundaries isn't about being mean or selfish; **it's about knowing your worth and keeping things balanced in your relationships.**

When you communicate your boundaries the right way, it helps others understand what's okay with you and what's not.

## DIGITAL BOUNDARIES

It is way too easy to just put up a post and not really think thoroughly of the full impact. **Think about how posts will affect your privacy and how you feel.** In addition (this will probably be common sense to you) but be careful about adding people you don't know or chatting with "randoms" online. Keep on the safe side.

**Too much screen time is not good for your mental health.** The Yale School of Medicine did a study on 5,000 teens. The study found the more time a teen spent on digital technology the higher the chances that teen would develop depression and anxiety in coming years. Excessive screentime increases sense of loneliness, FOMO (fear of missing out) and decreases life satisfaction and self-esteem. Teens who spent more time than average on non-screen activities were more likely to be happier. So bottom line, try to also set a limit on how much time you spend staring at screens. Make sure you're still living in the real world, too.

## START BY TALKING IT OUT AT HOME

Getting the hang of boundaries begins right at home. **Talk to your fam about how you're feeling and why boundaries matter, so everybody's on the same page.** Set up some ground rules for things like personal space and privacy, and make sure you can talk things out.

**Are there any boundaries you want to discuss at home? If so, what are they?**

_____

_____

_____

_____

_____

Having open and active chats about boundaries not only helps you say what you need but also gets others to see where you're coming from and why your boundaries matter. **To sum up, having good boundaries is all about looking out for yourself.** It's how you make sure your feelings and your body stay safe, keep your relationships healthy, and boost your confidence, self-worth, and personal growth. Trust your gut, speak up about your boundaries in a respectful but firm way. You are in control of living as your true self and keeping the right people around you. Make sure you set and stick to your own healthy boundaries to feel good and keep growing. Always remember, you've got the right to put up limits that keep you safe and make sure your needs are met.

## Chapter Seven

# GROUP VIBES: FITTING IN WHILE STANDING OUT

Whether you are in a community you choose or in ones that you are in by default, like your class, team, or anything else, there is NO doubt that, at times, it's a confusing world of trying to fit into a group while at the same time trying to be yourself.

Especially as a teenager, the need to be accepted and have friends is super important, but I will show you ways you don't have to give up who you are just to fit in. This chapter is about handling group situations without losing your true self. **We'll talk about when to go with the flow or be your unique self and how to handle peer pressure.**

## GETTING GROUP DYNAMICS WITHOUT LOSING YOURSELF

In any group environment, it is easy to get caught up trying to conform and lose who you are. Remember, being yourself and embracing your uniqueness adds to the diversity and benefits the group. To maintain your authenticity, keep these things in mind.

## SOUL SEARCH

As we have already started to do in this book, taking some time to dig deep and figure out what matters to you, your ideas, your thoughts, and your voice is super important to standing solid in a group setting. This self-discovery will be your North Star, guiding you in making choices that are right for you.

This self-reflection is the solid reliable ground you can stand on when keeping yourself intact while still being part of the group.

**Recap some interesting new things you have found out about yourself from reading this book and going through some of the exercises.**

_____

_____

_____

_____

# OWN YOUR UNIQUENESS

As I mentioned before, your uniqueness is your superpower. Own it. Embrace your quirks and talents, and understand the value of being yourself. **Build up faith in yourself**, which will help you hold strong in the face of outside influences and keep your realness in place when you are in a group.

**Name a talent or strength of yours that gave you more confidence in a specific group setting.**

_____

_____

**Explain how has having this talent or strength given you more confidence?**

_____

_____

_____

_____

# SET YOUR LIMITS

Define your personal boundaries and let people know where you stand if you need to. Remember that sacrificing your values or beliefs just to fit in can lead to a loss of self-respect and feelings of not feeling good about yourself. By drawing your lines, you can move through group dynamics while keeping your true self together.

Name a previous situation in a group setting when someone overstepped your boundaries, and you DIDN'T speak up!

_____

_____

_____

_____

Knowing your value system NOW, what would you do different in the same scenario?

_____

_____

_____

_____

# WHEN TO BLEND IN AND WHEN TO STAND OUT

Life is about balance, and group vibes are the same. Fitting in is about striking the right amount of blending in and being yourself. **Understand Group Radar. Take some time to tune into the group vibes** and figure out what they are about. Observe how they are interacting, talking, and showing themselves. This will help you adapt smoothly without losing yourself in the process. **Is there some common ground?** Look for stuff you all tend to gravitate to, like the same hobbies, interests, or values. Focusing on things you have in common allows you to make connections and feel like you belong while still being you.

**Describe a recent group situation where it was more helpful to first step back and "read" the room**

_____

_____

_____

_____

_____

**Did you find any "common ground(s)" of the group? If so, what were they?**

_____

_____

_____

_____

_____

**If there was common ground, from your observations, describe how and if it united the group?**

_____

_____

_____

_____

_____

**Did the common ground make YOU feel included? Write about your experience.**

_____

_____

_____

_____

_____

## ❙ BE YOU, STAND OUT

Don't be afraid to show off your quirks, talents, and thoughts. Bring your fresh view to the table and politely challenge the status quo when it makes sense. Let your presence in the group show how awesome, enlightening, and helpful it is to be different and for the entire group to be diverse.

**What do you think is your GREATEST talent or strength and why?**

_____

_____

_____

_____

# HOW TO HANDLE PEER PRESSURE WITHOUT A MELTDOWN

Peer pressure can really mess with your mind and lead you to face making tough decisions and lots of emotional drama. But the goal here is stand your ground and not let it shake you up. Here are some tips:

## TRUST YOURSELF

Boost your self-confidence by knowing your own worth and who you are inside. Remember, YOUR choices should come from your own beliefs and values, not what everyone else thinks.

## HANG WITH THE RIGHT CREW. BE AWARE OF FLAME BLOWER OUTTERS

> **"You cannot change the people around you, but you can change the people you choose to be around."**
> — *Joshua Millburn*

Surround yourself with friends who support and lift you up. Find friends who appreciate you for who you are and create a safe, supportive, and positive vibe.

**Be aware of flame blow outters.** What I mean by that is everyone has their own inner light, right? **There are some people who tend to be the FIRST ones to put you down or throw cold water on something positive.** For example, say that you got a part in a play that you really wanted. Some negative friends might say, "Theater is so geeky," or "What a dumb play." Those are flame blow outters. **You want to be surrounded by people who protect and support your light... who offer congrats for your wins, not put you down or get jealous.**

**Think of a scenario when a "friend" was a flame blower outter. Write it out and explain how it made you feel.**

_____

_____

_____

_____

_____

Now think of the opposite. Write of a time when a friend really cheered and supported you on and how that made you feel.

_____

_____

_____

_____

## SPEAK UP

Being the "odd opinion out" can feel awkward and really tough in a group situation even if you know it's the right thing to do. Learn to stand your ground and say what's what when you need to. **Practice saying "no" or speaking your mind with respect but firmness, and don't give in to stuff that messes with your well-being or things that aren't right for you.**

**Write about a recent scenario where you had to stand up for yourself, say no because it wasn't right for you.**

_____

_____

_____

_____

_____

**How did it make you feel knowing you did the right thing for yourself?**

_____

_____

_____

_____

## GET BACK UP

Reach out to grown-ups, mentors, or friends you trust when things get rough. They can give you different angles and ideas on dealing with peer pressure.

**Remember, keeping your cool in group situations while staying true to yourself takes practice.** But by being you, understanding how groups work, and handling peer pressure like a champ, you can get through any social scene.

*Chapter Eight*

# MAKING GREAT FRIENDS AND BEING ONE

"Each friend represents a world in us, a world possibly not born until they arrive, and it is only by this meeting that a new world is born."
— *Anais Nin*

When I was growing up, friends were the top two, if not the top priority of my teenage years. Yes, I should do well in school, yes, your family is important, but friends were really, really important during those years. This goes for a lot of teens. **Friends are the family you choose.** They are the people who support, understand, and share experiences with you. But how do you go about making friends and being a really great friend yourself? In this chapter, we will explore how to meet, start, and build lasting great friendships.

I love this saying, **"Most things you want in life happen on the other side of fear."** That means when you just go for it and overcome your fear of many things, a new world opens up. This is the same for developing new friendships.

## BE YOUR NATURAL, AMAZING SELF

"Just be yourself, there is no one better."
— *Taylor Swift*

**The BEST way to start making friends is to be yourself.** People say this all the time, "be yourself," but it is absolutely true. This just means you don't need to pretend to be anyone else but you. Being yourself around brand-new people isn't all that easy, but it really is the way to go. **When you are more yourself...guess what? You are funnier, more relatable, relaxed, and more confident. Being real is key.** When you are true to yourself, you attract friends who appreciate and accept you for who you are. Friendships should be based on genuine connections, not on always trying to fit in or being someone you're not.

## ▍NEED A PLACE TO START?

The obvious easiest places to start making friends are by playing a team sport, joining a club, taking part in extracurricular activities, or in class. Seems pretty basic. If you are the right age, maybe get a part-time job where you are around some of your peers. Having a part-time job can also give you a sense of independence and purpose.

I found having a part-time job as a teen great in so many ways. First, I didn't have to ask my parents for money if I wanted to buy something (and the follow-up back and forth comments from them that "I didn't need it"). With a job, I worked, saved up my money and bought what I wanted. Secondly, I felt a sense of accomplishment. I bought what I wanted with the money that *I* earned. *My* decision from *my* job. Making your own coin boosts your confidence. Third, I got to meet some really cool people along the way. I met some great friends I would have otherwise never met if I hadn't had that part-time job. Fourth, I appreciated my parents and the concept of work more. I had a part-time job to buy things I wanted. My parents worked all day to cover the bills for our entire family. This allowed me to have a teeny glimpse into their working lives.

# BE APPROACHABLE, LOOK APPROACHABLE AND WELCOMING

Positive and joyful people tend to attract others naturally. Smile. Look like someone who is open to having a conversation. **People tend to gravitate toward someone who has a friendly, open, upbeat, and positive presence.**

**Write about a scenario where someone you met had such an open positive vibe, you wanted to get to know them better?**

_____

_____

_____

_____

_____

**On a scale of 1-10, how open and friendly do you think you come across?**

_____

# GO AHEAD. INTRODUCE YOURSELF

Most people feel weird introducing themselves to people they have never spoken to before. This goes for adults too, but we may be better at hiding it. If everyone who felt awkward waited for someone else to come up and speak to them, then most of us would be standing around by ourselves for a really, really long time. It all has to start somewhere. And why not you to get it rolling? Trust me...you can do it.

Get into a habit of saying hello first. If you aren't comfortable then practice. Saying hi first gives a vibe of confidence. I understand some people are just more introverted than others, and it is tough for introverted people to start conversations. Introducing yourself can be a really big step outside of your comfort zone. Just start small, step by step. Like most things in life, the more you do it, the easier it will become. In the beginning, it may feel strange, but it will get easier with more practice. Making great friends is worth the risk of stepping outside your comfort zone.

## STARTING A CONVERSATION

How do you start a conversation and keep it going? **Start by asking open-ended questions** instead of asking questions with only yes or no answers or super quick answers. If you are trying to speak (especially to someone shy), yes, no, or one-word answers will not get you far. So, ask questions that spark more conversations. An example is, "What did you think of that class?" Ask for their opinion on something. You can even ask for their input on the homework. This not only opens the door for a conversation but also shows that you value their opinion.

**Write down some other examples of open ended questions you can think of.**

_____

_____

_____

_____

_____

## SHOW REAL, GENUINE INTEREST IN THEIR THOUGHTS AND THE CONVERSATION

Come across like you care about what they are saying. Make eye contact. Don't mutter your words. Remember, this is a two-way street, so let the other person speak freely, and don't try to dominate the conversation because you are nervous or trying to just get your point across.

## FIND SOME COMMON GROUND

"One friend with whom you have a lot in common is better than three with whom you struggle to find things to talk about."
— *Mindy Kaling*

Now that we have found your likes and dislikes, etc., you can start with people who may share the same common interests as you. If you meet new people, find out if you share some common ground.

If you are new to the school, fresh to the group, or new to the environment, let them know you are new. You can even ask for their rundown on your new situation. If the conversation seems to be going well, then go ahead and ask for their contact info so you can keep in touch or would like more of their input. Put yourself out there.

## TRY THIS IDEA IF YOU ARE SUPER SHY

If you are very introverted, you may have to do something a bit more extreme to get you out of your comfort zone. This may sound scary at first, but it could be an excellent way to help bring you out of your shell. **Think about taking a teen improv class.** What is an improv class? "Improv" is short for improvisation. Improv is basically a class that is spontaneous theater. There is no script. Scenes are created by suggestions from a teacher, the group, or even from the audience. Then, the actors (i.e., people in the class) have to perform a made-up scene on the spot. What's great about improv class is that it makes you think on your feet, it is a group effort, allows you to have fun "failing" in a safe space without judgment and is often hilarious because you have no idea what is going to come out of someone's mouth. You are also trying something new every time. The process can be really fun, interesting, challenging, and you can develop courage and confidence.

If there isn't a teen improv class around you or it is not your vibe, think about theater, public speaking, or doing something in front of an audience. This is what I would call the "medicine ball" technique. A medicine ball is much heavier than a regular ball. Basically, tackle something that you consider to be tougher, harder, and much more outside your comfort zone in order to be able to tackle something average with ease. **When you go outside of what you think are your limits, then your limits end up changing.**

## THIS WON'T WORK EVERY TIME

Sometimes there will be people who just don't feel like having a conversation. Don't ever take that personally. Everyone has their own stuff going on that they don't show the world. If your conversation doesn't seem to be landing the way you want, it is OK to move on. It happens to the best of us. You did great, and move on.

I know this may sound cheesy, but you can also do some role-play with people in your family or someone you trust and practice how you would start conversations. Practice will make you less anxious. Prep some questions you can start role-playing with.

## UNDERSTAND FRIENDSHIP IS A GRADUAL PROGRESSION

Friendships usually aren't as simple as introducing yourself, you connect, and then instant deep friendships develop right away. All friendships take time and go through emotional layers. Everyone tests people out on an "acquaintance" level...like first layer, is when you meet someone in a class or sports, and you both decide you want to get to know each other. Then, once past this phase, you enter the "friends" stage and then, with more time, the "good friends" stage. There is usually some level of earned trust at the "good friends" stage. Then there is the "best friend" zone where you can be the most vulnerable, authentic self and have a real sense of loyalty.

**It's essential to also understand that friendships go through changes and evolve over time.** People grow, get new interests, move, and sometimes drift apart. It's important to accept these changes as a normal part of life and recognize that not all friendships are meant to last forever. You can have a really close friendship that only lasts the summer or a couple of years because you went to the same school or were on the same team. Maybe someone had to pack up and move away. Or maybe you just drift apart.

On the other hand, you can develop friendships that last decades and a lifetime. Friendships have varied time frames, ups and downs, just like phases of life. So don't stress if some friendships don't last as long as you expected. Be open to changes. This also allows you to recognize and cherish the cool connections you have while you have them, live in the moment, while also being open to developing new friendships.

## THE DIFFERENCE BETWEEN GOOD AND BAD FRIENDSHIPS

What makes a friendship cool or not cool? A solid friendship? That's all about respecting each other, trusting each other, and having each other's backs. Good friends get your vibe, accept you, cheer you on, and are there to listen when things get rough. You can talk about anything with them, and it's straight-up (while still being respectful) and positive. They protect and support your inner light.

But a bad friendship? That's a whole different story. It's when someone's always playing mind games, you can't really trust them, and everything just feels kind of negative. If a friend makes you feel bad, oversteps your limits, or always brings drama, that's not good. It's super important to know when a friendship is toxic and to figure out what to do – either talk it out or, sometimes, you just gotta keep your distance. If a friendship keeps bringing you down and makes you feel bad, listen to your inner guide. It could be time to walk away.

## HOW TO BE A GOOD FRIEND

This is probably one of the most important life lessons because friends are not only super important in your teenage years but for the rest of your life.

Trust me, when you are going through life's highs and lows and everything in the middle, it is essential to have your people around. So it's important for you to know what it takes to be a good friend. Once you have developed good friends, these are lifelong tips to keep in mind. Think about what type of friend you would want!

## HAVE THEIR BACK

Be there for your friends, no matter what. If they're going through tough times or need someone to stand up for them, you're there.

## KEEP IT REAL

Be honest with them, not in a harsh way, but in a 'telling it like it is because you care' way. You can be really honest without being mean.

## LISTEN UP

When they talk, actually listen. Don't just wait for your turn to speak. Get what they're saying and where they're coming from. Put yourself in the other person's shoes.

## SPREAD THE HYPE

Be their cheerleader. Celebrate their wins, big or small, and hype them up when they're feeling down.

## RESPECT THEIR SPACE

Understand that everyone needs a little space sometimes. It's cool to do your own thing and let them do theirs.

## KEEP SECRETS SECRET

If they trust you with a secret, keep it locked down. No sharing, no matter what, unless it involves extreme situations like their or others' safety or well-being. When you blab about someone's deepest moments that they have shared with you in confidence, you come across as someone who has little self-control and can't be trusted. It's hurtful.

## DON'T BE A GHOST

Stay in touch, even when life gets busy. Shoot a text, give them a call, or reach out for a catch-up. Just let them know you're thinking of them.

## DITCH THE DRAMA

Keep it chill. If there's a small issue, don't make it a big deal. And if there's a big issue, talk it out calmly.

## BE YOU

Just be yourself around them. The best thing in the world is to be around people that you can be completely yourself with. Life is so much fun and fulfilling that way. Good friends love you for who you are, not who you pretend to be.

**Write about a time where you were completely yourself with someone. How did it make you feel?**

_____

_____

_____

_____

_____

_____

_____

What are the qualities YOU would want in a friend?

_____

_____

_____

_____

_____

Describe in detail what your IDEAL friend would be like?

_____

_____

_____

_____

_____

## PICK THE RIGHT TRIBE. IT'S IMPORTANT

"You are the product of the five people you spend the most time with."
— *Tim Ferris*

Do you know the most important factor in who you become? It is not your background, your race, your gender, your education, how much money you grew up with, or even where you were raised. **More than any single factor in determining who you become is who you surround yourself with.**

Studies show this time and time again, so I am not going to bore you with a ton of data. **Even though you have a mind of your own, most people are**

**highly influenced by the behaviors, beliefs, habits, and the mindsets of people around them.** So when you pick your people to associate with, remind yourself to pick people who will be good influences on you. Surround yourself with positive, empathetic, helpful, and supportive people. Your tribe can bring you up and take you down. They will add to the beliefs you have about yourself and the world.

This doesn't mean dropping every single negative person in your life, and sometimes that is not realistic. But you can limit the time you spend with someone who just keeps dragging you down.

# Chapter Nine
## EMOTIONAL REGULATION

Figuring out all these big emotions during the teen years can be a roller coaster. But, if you keep at it, you can get amazing at handling and making sense of your feelings. Getting your feelings in check is super key to gaining more confidence, bouncing back from tough times, developing healthy relationships, cutting back stress, and just feeling better all around. There is some overlap of tips I talked about in the "Overcoming Emotional Monsters" chapter as they work here, too. In this chapter, I'll break down why it's good to keep an eye on your emotions and know when to just let things go, especially when those intense feelings hit you. We'll also dive into handling bullies and why forgiveness helps heal your emotional vibes and set you free.

## WHAT AM I EXACTLY FEELING?

**To begin this journey, step one is to pinpoint exactly WHAT you're feeling.** When you start getting all these emotions, hit the pause button for a sec and try to work out exactly what that emotion is.

Is it anger, sadness, jealousy, embarrassment, or is it a mix of different emotions? Break it down and start figuring out which ones they are. Be honest with yourself. There is no point trying to fool yourself into thinking you aren't feeling something. You are human. Humans are meant to feel a whole range of emotions. If you feel jealous, then acknowledge it. If you feel embarrassed, acknowledge it. But find out what it is.

# WRITE IT OUT

You might wanna try keeping a journal and jot down what you are feeling. It's a great way to let out and sort through what you're dealing with. Plus, it helps you spot any patterns or things that set off your emotions. It's not just about tracking your mood swings. It's starting your road map for self-reflection and growing as a person.

# POSITIVE SELF

**As I mentioned before, make positive self-talk part of your daily routine.** Positive self-talk is not just cheesy whoo-whoo stuff. This will help you feel stronger and more together. The more you do this, the more you will realize how less "thrown off" you become when someone or some event tries to knock you down. You know you will get back up and be resilient. You know you can tackle anything that comes your way.

**Keep a list of positive affirmations around to remind yourself of your strengths, capabilities, and talents.** When negative thoughts start to infiltrate your mind, counter them with affirmations like "I am awesome no matter what anyone says" or "I have overcome challenges before, and I can do it again." Keep going back to these affirmations and repeat them a lot so they really sink in deep and start to change how you think. It's all about steering your mind toward being kind to yourself and staying positive.

**Write out some positive affirmations about yourself (also remember the Light Trick from Chapter 3).**

_____

_____

_____

_____

_____

_____

_____

## BREATHE

**Deep breathing is a real trick to chill out when stuff gets tough.** If you're feeling super overwhelmed or anxious, just close your eyes for a sec and pay attention to your breathing. Breathe in deep for four seconds, hold it for another four, and then let it out slowly for four seconds. Do this a few times and let your breath keep you in the present. Give it a shot. **It's like hitting the relax button, calming your nerves down, and helping you get a grip on your emotions.**

## FORGIVENESS. THIS IS A BIG ONE.

**"Forgiveness isn't approving what happened. It's choosing to rise above it."**

— _Robin Sharma_

Sometimes, we get so angry, and the emotion is big. **But as hard as it can be sometimes, don't hold grudges.** Holding grudges aren't good for you. This doesn't mean you are opening a door to being treated like a doormat when someone has wronged or taken advantage of it. This doesn't mean you are forgetting what happened either. You have your boundaries, and if you need to stay away or take a break for a bit, that is probably the right move.

**And there very well may be some things that can't be righted, some things that can't be undone, or things that should have been done that weren't. Some things just aren't fair, and some situations can't be made whole. But forgive.**

What I am saying is don't let the anger or the grudge eat at you, and don't hold on to hate and anger. This holds you back. Forgive, but you don't have to forget. That grudge energy spoils the vibe of moving forward. Let it go. **Holding onto grudges and anger tends to lock YOU up much more than the other person.** When you forgive, you set YOURSELF free. If anything, forgive other people just for your own sake.

**This forgiveness goes for you, too. This is a reminder to forgive yourself regularly for mistakes that you made. Know you can do better and learn from it.**

**Are there any people (even yourself) you think you should forgive? Write them down.**

_____

_____

_____

_____

# GRATITUDE

I find one of the best ways to "feel better" is by picking five things I am really grateful for. **It is actually hard to be really angry and truly grateful at the same time.** When you get frustrated, upset, or down, think of things you are truly grateful for, think about it, and feel it. Feeling real love or gratitude isn't ignoring the feelings you are actually feeling. **Love and gratitude allow you to feel those emotions but from a more productive healthy place to better process what is going on.** Write them out. It changes your mood quickly.

Write down five things you are grateful for in your life. **They could be big or small. Make sure they are your own thing.** Don't write down what you

SHOULD write but write down what you really feel on the inside. What are you grateful for?

_____

_____

_____

_____

_____

_____

_____

_____

## YOUR CHILL SPOT

Sometimes, you need an actual "chill space". Taking a break and finding a "peaceful spot" can be a quick go-to needed escape when emotions feel intense. Find a physical space, whether it's a cozy corner of your room, a quiet area in the library, or a peaceful outdoor spot, where you can retreat and regroup. This space should be free from distractions and allow you to immerse yourself in a calming atmosphere. Think about bringing headphones and listening to chill music or even positive podcasts...whatever calms you. Taking some solid time just for yourself to unwind and unplug can seriously help cut down on stress, keep your emotions in check, and give your brain a much-needed recharge.

**What is your chill spot?**

_____

_____

# GET MOVING

Getting into a workout routine is an amazing way to keep your emotions in check and feel all-around awesome. When you exercise, your body pumps out endorphins, those feel-good natural chemicals that crank up your happiness and lower stress. Find a way to move that you enjoy, like running, swimming, dancing, or yoga, and make it a big deal in your daily grind. Regular exercise doesn't just boost your mood; it also improves your physical health, which is a massive win for your confidence and how you feel about yourself.

**What is your favorite way to get moving?**

_____

_____

_____

# MAYBE YOU JUST NEED TO TALK IT OUT (WITHOUT JUDGMENT)

All this stuff about self-reflection and keeping your emotions in check is good, but sometimes, when things get way too intense, it's super helpful to talk to someone you trust. Look for someone who's a good listener – like a really close friend, a family member, or maybe a counselor – **someone who'll hear you out without judging.** Just letting it all out and sharing your feelings can lift a ton of weight off your shoulders. Plus, getting someone else's point of view can clear things up and help you deal with all those complicated emotions. Remember, getting the hang of managing your emotions and figuring out who you are doesn't happen overnight. It takes practice and patience. Cut yourself some slack while you work through all the ups and downs. By using these strategies daily and digging deep to understand yourself, you will build a rock-solid base of emotional strength and self-confidence. **And trust me, that's gonna make a big difference in every part of your life.**

*Chapter Ten*

# HOW TO COMMUNICATE EFFECTIVELY

Effective communication is really vital. Being able to talk things out and really get your point across is a big step toward feeling confident and keeping relationships solid, not just as a teen but for the rest of your life. Having great communication skills means you know HOW to say what you want to say, are actively listening and understanding where people are coming from.

## SAY WHAT YOU MEAN, BUT WITH RESPECT

When communicating with someone, it's key to keep it direct, real, and straight-up. **Say what you think and feel. It's just as important to think about how your words will land with them. Be respectful.** This means picking your words wisely and not getting aggressive or rude. Try to "feel" their point of view from a bigger picture perspective. **Imagine being in their place – how would you want someone to talk to you? You want to convey your thoughts respectfully, so the other person doesn't feel rejected.** When everyone is respectful in a convo, you sort stuff out much better.

For example, say you are leading a class project, and you're getting some opinions for a topic. You start putting out feelers from your group on which topic to choose. A friend gives you an idea, but you really don't think it's a good fit. Scrap the "I am right", "You are wrong" vibe. This gives an air of superiority which can come across dismissive and hurtful.

**My experience is the act of showing gratitude for their input graciously can lessen any sense of rejection, even if you disagree.** So instead of saying "Nah, I don't think that's a good idea", say instead, "I really appreciate that you took the time to give me some ideas; helps take some stuff off my plate!

We might be looking for something with a different theme, but I'll add your idea to the list and think it over". You have no idea if that person took a bit of courage to speak up. This type of interaction encourages other people to open up without feeling you will squash their thoughts. They also gain more respect for you as a leader because you were able to navigate the conversation smoothly.

**If you DON'T know what to say and it is a hard conversation, then sit with your thoughts for a bit.** Ask yourself this very pointed question: how would YOU like to have someone say to you what you're about to say? What are the words, the tone, the body language, the energy that you would want someone to have with for the message to land better with you?

## DON'T EXPECT SOMEONE TO READ YOUR MIND

**A LOT of arguments start with someone not understanding where the other person is coming from or misunderstanding what the other person is trying to say.** The funny thing is, many people EXPECT the other person to get where they are coming from automatically (basically being able to read their mind), but at the same time, that same person doesn't take the time to see the situation from the other person's shoes. You see the problem? **Most of the time, people get upset with the other person for the same exact thing they are doing (not seeing it from their point of view).**

Sometimes, we feel like people should just KNOW what's going on in your head, right? But the truth is, everyone's different, and they can't always guess what you're thinking. So much drama starts just because someone thinks the other person could read their mind.

So, to resolve this, **it's much better to just own how you talk and directly say what you need, what you want, and what's exactly bothering you.** Don't dodge around it. **Also, as I mentioned before try to use 'I' statements to talk about your feelings.** Remember,  it keeps things from sounding like you're blaming or accusing anyone, and it makes it easier for people to get where you're coming from.

For example, instead of saying, " YOU are not being fair," " YOU are inconsiderate," or " YOU are not paying attention," you are better off saying, "When this happens, I feel like I am not being treated as equally," " I feel that my feelings aren't being taken into consideration, "I feel like there are other things on your mind." Using "I" or "I feel" just sounds less harsh and less blaming while still getting your point across.

**Anytime you LESSEN the BLAME factor, the other person feels less attacked and more likely to listen.** When people hear blame, many will just hear, "You are a horrible person." No one likes to feel attacked, and **some people actually emotionally shut down** (i.e., won't listen to whatever you have to say, even though it is completely valid) if they feel attacked.

**Write about a scenario when there was an argument or a fight you had because there was a miscommunication or misunderstanding**

_____

_____

_____

_____

_____

**How do you think the scenario would have been different if there was clearer communication?**

_____

_____

_____

## BE THOUGHTFUL AND RESPECT OTHER PEOPLE'S TIME AND VIEWS

Even though it's tough sometimes, we have to really listen to people. What does that mean? It's about showing respect by actually paying attention to what they're saying and caring about their opinions, **even if they differ from yours.** Have talks without cutting them off or hogging the convo, and let everyone get their point across. By being empathetic and trying to see things from their point of view, you can have real and open discussions. **It also helps if you aren't asking questions that lead to just 'yes' or 'no' answers.** Have them elaborate. That way, people can dive deep into their thoughts and feelings. Both sides can better understand each other.

## IF THINGS GET HEATED, TAKE A MOMENT TO COOL DOWN… THEN SPEAK

In situations where emotions get heated, or conflicts come up, **it is important to take a step back and give yourself time to calm down before responding. Reacting impulsively or super fast in the heat of the moment can lead to misunderstandings or hurtful words that can really damage relationships.** Take deep breaths, count to ten, or do a calming activity to regroup. When you are calmer, approach the situation again with a clearer mind and start again into a more thoughtful and straightforward chat.

When you get angry, your emotions are really raging. What you think you want to say may sound very legit to you in that moment, but when you are speaking from this angry space, there will be more harm done than good. And some things you say will be very hard to take back. Trust me, it's always better to step away when things get this heated and revisit the convo after things calm down.

I know when I get SO upset about something I can speak from a place of hurt. This place of hurt can say some mean things out of the gate. This place of hurt doesn't usually see the full picture. To make any situation better you NEED to see the full picture. **Think of it like a painting. You need to step farther back to see it in full.** Same thing with disagreements. This takes time and detachment. So, take a breather, walk around the block or whatever you need to cool off.

If you want to take it a step further, and as hard as it may seem in this moment, close your eyes and send LOVE to yourself and that person, or even the incident. Feel it. **Whenever I take a moment to do this, I start feeling better. USUALLY, the situation also takes on a better air.** Remember, if something was done to you, this is not giving approval to the situation, it is allowing you to view things from a healthier perspective.

## PRACTICE BETTER NON-VERBAL COMMUNICATION

Good communication and talking aren't just about the words you say or write. Body language, how your voice sounds, and the look on your face say a ton too. **Be aware of the vibes you're giving off without words.** For example, if you're saying 'sorry' but sounding mad or rushing through it, **you're really not apologizing at all.** You're just trying to get it over with without actually meaning it. People read that. So, you gotta try again. The way you sound, your focus, and how you carry yourself affect how your message is received. And don't just think about your own signals – check out the other person's too. The more you understand these non-verbal cues, the better you'll be at getting your point across and understanding others.

## GET CLEAR AND PROVIDE FEEDBACK

As I mentioned above, tons of misunderstandings happen when information doesn't get clarified or when people just assume. To avoid this, actively seek to clearly understand what the person is saying **by asking questions if**

**needed.** Many times, someone has no idea that they weren't being clear. This can happen in group settings too. **So speak up if you don't understand something.** There could be other people around you wondering the same thing, and the speaker may not have any clue about this. You could be helping the entire group. As a participant, it is also up to you to make sure you are on the same page as the person communicating. Also, again, be respectful. **It is better to comment on a specific behavior versus attacking the person. That never goes anywhere except somewhere negative.**

**Write about a time you or someone spoke up in a group to get clarity from the speaker. Explain how and if it helped the group.**

_____

_____

_____

_____

_____

## GET CLEAR ON WRITTEN COMMUNICATION TOO

These days, we communicate way more through written communication than talking. To be honest, when I am texting back and forth, I sometimes forget I can pick up the phone and speak to them live instead of texting. So this makes written communication that much more important to be clear and considerate. When you're writing something, take a moment to double-check it and make sure it says what you want it to say to avoid any confusion. If things get complicated or touchy, it also could be best to talk in person or over the phone so you can really understand each other.

**What steps do you think you can take right now to get clearer on your overall communication?**

_____

_____

_____

_____

_____

Getting great at communicating is a skill that you have to work on and fine-tune. It might be challenging, but if you make a conscious effort, you can take your communication to a higher level. Whether it's with your friends, fam, teachers, or even with people you'll work with later...communicating clearly, with respect, and actually listening is super important. It helps build solid relationships, sort out issues without the drama, and improve every part of your life.

# CULTURAL SENSITIVITY

In a world where we're all connected and diverse, it's super important to respect different backgrounds and views. **Keep in mind that where someone is from often impacts how they talk, what they care about, how they see the world, and what they believe. Be aware of these differences and avoid jumping to conclusions or making assumptions.** When interacting with people from other places or cultures, try to understand and appreciate the differences. Take a little time to learn about their background, customs, manners, and how they like to communicate. That way, you can make everyone feel included when interacting with them.

I grew up in Ohio. We didn't have a lot of diversity in school, so I grew up not knowing a lot about other backgrounds or cultures. This was before social media and the internet was in its infancy so there wasn't a free flow of info. A girl just moved to my school from South Africa. She talked differently, dressed differently, and I thought she was the coolest person ever. I never met anyone from South Africa before. It seemed like another planet to me. I know this sounds ignorant, but I asked her if there were a bunch of animals walking around where she lived. I was just so clueless - I wanted her to tell me everything. I had an idea in my head that it was like being dropped in *Jumanji*.

She explained that she grew up in a city and it was common to come across people who spoke eight to eleven languages. She told me about the political environment, the big number of different cultures, the beaches, the class system, the food, how people viewed the US... everything. My impression of what I thought South Africa was like was so different from what she told me it was *actually* like. Until I met someone face to face and asked her what life was like there, I never would have known how off my assumptions were.

It is essential if you have questions about something outside of your world to take the time to sit down and have a conversation with people about their background, their experiences to gain REAL knowledge. Have them unpack it for you. Books and movies are great but having real life conversations gives you a 3D picture that is relatable, digestible, and emotionally connecting.

This is one of the reasons why I love to travel so much. In full form, right in front of you, we get to see how other people live, communicate, how they dress, how they interact and what is important to them. I get to see and appreciate differences in other cultures way more than reading a book or on TV, while at the same time, highlighting how similar we all are in ways too. If you get a chance to travel and explore different cultures, go for it. It really is one of life's greatest and coolest adventures.

*Chapter Eleven*

# HOW TO SPEAK UP AND SPEAK OUT

Having the confidence to speak your mind and stand up for what you believe takes courage, practice and is a really important skill to have. This skill allows you to share your thoughts, stick up for yourself, and be an active participant in the conversation. In this chapter, we're diving deep into how to do it confidently and effectively.

## BE TRUE TO YOURSELF AND YOUR OWN VOICE. BE YOU, STAY TRUE

**First things first, always respect your own beliefs and thoughts.** It is important to VALUE your own beliefs and perspectives. Don't feel pressured to go along with the crowd if it doesn't align with your values. Having a voice and expressing your thoughts and opinions is powerfully important in building a dynamic life for yourself and is key in shaping it. But, when you disagree, do it with respect and an open mind. Let others finish their say and as always, try to get where they're coming from.

## LISTEN ACTIVELY AND EMPATHETICALLY. HEAR 'EM OUT

Speaking your mind isn't just hearing yourself talk and ignoring what others think. It's important to really hear what they have to say. When you're talking, keep an open mind. Put yourself in their shoes. Doing this makes for better conversations, helps you connect on a deeper level and makes you smarter. When you actively listen, it shows you respect them, and it makes room for both of you to understand and learn from each other.

## DO YOUR RESEARCH. DO YOUR HOMEWORK

Getting ready is the secret to speaking up with confidence and making your point stick. **Before you dive into a topic, do some homework.** Get the facts straight and look at things from different angles. Dig into the subject, learn as much as you can, and come up with solid reasons to back up your thoughts. When you've got evidence, data, and good reasons on your side, your words will carry more weight, and your talks will be more worthwhile. **Knowledge helps you build trust, and it makes it easier to deal with any arguments that come your way.** When you know your stuff, your voice carries more weight, and you can handle counterarguments like a champ.

## MASTER GOOD COMMUNICATION TRICKS WE TALKED ABOUT. TALK THE TALK

When sharing your thoughts, it's key to use your communication moves to get your message across strong, clear, and confident. Look people in the eye, use body language that fits the situation, and talk like you mean it. **Keep it short and sweet, and organize your ideas in a way that makes sense.** Skip the long-winded or super-technical stuff and go for words that anyone can get. If you speak in a way that's easy to understand and convincing, you'll be great at getting your point across and getting other people to join in on a real conversation.

## GET GOOD AT REALLY LISTENING AND RESPECTING DIFFERENT POINTS OF VIEW. LISTEN AND LEARN

Good communication works both ways. You've got to be a good talker, but more importantly, you've got to be a great listener. When people respond or give you feedback, pay attention and get into how they are thinking. Even if they see things differently, show that you understand and respect their ideas. Show you care. Be open to learning new stuff or changing your own views when you hear something new or see things in a different light because of the new information. When you have open chats like this, it helps everyone understand each other better and work together.

**Write a scenario when you learned something new by just listening to someone else's point of view that was different from yours?**

_____

_____

_____

_____

## CHOOSE THE RIGHT TIME AND PLACE. TIME IT RIGHT

When you're about to speak up, think about when and where it's best to do it. Pick the right moment and place to be heard and respected. Timing and the situation can really make a difference in how your message comes across. Take into account what's going on, who's there, and what might happen because of what you say. Think about the situation, who's involved, and what your words could mean. Try to have a constructive talk instead of starting a fight, and look for things you can agree on. **When you carefully choose when and where to talk, you make it more likely that your conversation will be helpful and make sense.**

## CRUSH FEAR AND DOUBT

Speaking up, especially in challenging or controversial situations, can be scary. It's natural to experience fear, and self-doubt, and feel nervous or unsure. However, it is important to remember that your opinions and views matter. **Build your self-confidence by practicing speaking up in smaller settings,** such as with close friends or family. Each small step will help you develop the courage to voice your thoughts in more challenging situations.

Remember, your voice deserves to be heard, and the value you bring to the conversation is significant. Your thoughts count!

**Is there something you want to speak up about that you haven't built up the courage to talk about yet?**

_____

_____

_____

_____

## STAND UP FOR WHAT MATTERS AND WHAT YOU BELIEVE IN

Speaking your mind isn't just about personal stuff—it's also about supporting causes that mean something to you. Whether it's standing up for fairness, the environment, or whatever lights you up, find ways to show your support and make an impact. Get involved with groups that care about the same things and add your voice to the conversation. When you team up with others and spread the word, your voice gets louder, and you can really make a difference. Remember, you have the power to bring about change by speaking up for what you believe in. Being part of a movement and raising awareness can amplify your voice and help you bring about change. Know that your voice has the power to make a difference.

Remember that speaking up and speaking out is a lifelong adventure in getting to know yourself better. It's a skill that can help you handle all sorts of social and work situations. Keep at it, have faith in your own voice, and recognize the good you can do by sharing your thoughts and standing up for what you care about. **But never forget to be respectful and willing to hear other points of view so we can all keep talking and understanding each other.** When you speak up, you're not just helping yourself grow—you're also creating a place where everyone's voice matters, and that can lead to some really positive changes.

# Chapter Twelve

## DEALING WITH DRAMA AND DISAGREEMENTS

Dealing with drama and fights can be seriously tough and messy, and it really puts your patience and emotional energy to the test. Life can sometimes feel like a big web of complicated relationships, BUT in these hard times, we get a chance to grow and make our connections with others even stronger. Figuring out how to handle these situations without losing your cool and with a bit of wisdom is super important for keeping your relationships healthy, growing as a person, and staying sane. So, here are some good tips to help you get through all the drama and fights that might come your way.

## GET AT THE UNDERLYING MEANING

**Skillful communication is THE foundation of resolving disagreements.** Actively listening to the concerns, perspectives, and feelings of others is the first step toward establishing understanding and empathy. It involves not just hearing the words being spoken but also paying attention to nonverbal cues, subtle emotions, and underlying intentions.

**Try to understand what they are REALLY trying to say and why.** For example, when someone is upset with you about being late for something, **what they REALLY may be hurt about is**, "You aren't taking me, this event, this dinner, or whatever, that seriously. **I am getting the message that I am not that important to you and I feel disrespected". That is really the underlying meaning.** So address it. " I am so sorry; I know this is important, and I will do better next time." Instead of saying. "I am only 20 minutes late", or "Why is this such a big deal?" **look for the underlying issue they may be upset about.**

Practice listening without judgment, interrupting, or over-analyzing. By genuinely showing interest and respect for others' viewpoints, you create a safe space for open dialogue and collaboration.

## EMBRACE EMOTIONAL INTELLIGENCE. GET IN TOUCH WITH YOUR FEELINGS

Being emotionally smart is a big deal when it comes to handling fights. **It begins with knowing yourself, understanding your OWN feelings, what sets you off, and any personal biases you might have.**

**Many people go through day and life shoving their feelings down and not fully addressing them.** Think about how often you do this every day. When feelings come up, recognize what they are, how they are triggered, and, if needed, what to do about them (remember the chapter on emotional monsters). This doesn't have to be just negative, heavy emotions. Also take note of the joy, happiness, and feelings of confidence. **The more aware you are of your emotions, the smarter you become in regulating your life.**

When you recognize and own your emotions, you can deal with conflicts more clearly and sensibly. But it's not just about you—emotional intelligence also means getting what other people are feeling and being able to put yourself in their shoes. When you really understand where they're coming from, it makes it easier to talk and connect with them on a deeper level, which leads to more compassion and teamwork.

## STOP AND THINK IT THROUGH

**When you're dealing with a big argument, don't just dive in headfirst.** Take a breather and think it over. Take a good look at how you're feeling, what's going on in your head, and what you believe about the whole thing.

Ask yourself what really matters to you and how you can work things out in a way that sticks with your own values. This self-reflection stuff helps you come at conflicts with a clear plan and make sure your reactions are all about staying true to who you are.

## BE NON-CONFRONTATIONAL

It is important to solve problems without getting all up in someone's face. It's about understanding each other and talking with compassion. **Again, instead of blaming or judging, express how you feel and what you need.** Try to find solutions that work for everyone. Talk about what you see, how you feel, what you need, why it's important to you, and what you'd like to create a vibe of trust and empathy that helps sort things out.

## BE CURIOUS

**When there's a disagreement, it's a chance for some real talk and personal growth.** When you're talking it out, **think about learning something** and having a helpful conversation **instead of trying to win or lose. Come at it with a curious mindset**, trying to learn and understand what the other person is saying instead of just trying to prove you're right. This way, you make it easier for everyone to work together, learn together, and find a solution that works for everyone.

## WIN-WIN MINDSET

The goal of conflict resolution should never be to defeat or "win" over the other person. **Think about both sides winning.** When you're trying to solve a problem, don't make it about beating the other person. Aim for a solution where everyone feels like they've been heard, respected, and happy with how things turn out. It's about working together and showing respect to each other. When you switch from a "me against you" mindset to a "let's work this out together" mindset, you make it easier to find solutions that keep the peace and make your relationships stronger.

## FINDING MIDDLE GROUND

**When you're working through arguments, it's important to understand the difference between finding compromising and straight-up sacrificing.** Compromising means finding a spot in the middle where everyone makes some changes and gives up a little to improve both sides. **Sacrificing,** on the other hand, means giving up things that are really important to you, **which can make you feel pretty resentful or like you're being taken for granted. Aim for compromises that respect your own boundaries and keep everyone's core values and well-being intact.**

## BOOST YOUR EMOTIONAL TOUGHNESS

When you're in a fight, it can bring up emotions like anger, frustration, or sadness. **But you can build up your emotional strength to handle these emotions in a good way.** Try self-care stuff like working out, keeping a journal, or talking to people you care about to help you recharge and deal with your feelings in a healthy way. When you work on your emotional toughness, you make yourself more resistant to the bad stuff that comes with conflicts, and you come out of it even stronger, smarter, and kinder.

## TAKE NOTES FROM YOUR PREVIOUS FIGHT EXPERIENCES

Even though fights can be super awkward, they can teach us some really useful stuff about ourselves, our connections with others, and where we can grow. **Once you've sorted out a conflict, give it some thought and see if you can spot any habits, things that set you off, or places where you can improve yourself.** Don't be too hard on yourself for any mistakes you've made, and promise yourself you'll learn from them. When you see disagreements as a chance to improve, you become more understanding, emotionally smart, and really good at talking to people.

**What are some valuable lessons you have learned from YOUR previous fight experiences?**

_____

_____

_____

_____

_____

_____

_____

## GET SOME OUTSIDE HELP WHEN THINGS GET TOUGH

Sometimes, fights can be really tricky, messy, emotionally exhausting, and painful. It can be hard to work things out on your own. When things get this rough, it's a good idea to reach out to a mentor or a pro, like a therapist, counselor, or conflict guru. They are like neutral referees who can guide you, give you a fresh view of things, and may help you resolve arguments better. They're good at creating a safe space where you can talk it out, get to what's really going on, and find ways to resolve arguments that actually work.

You know, how we deal with all the drama and fights says a lot about who we are and how strong our relationships are. If you focus on understanding your emotions, taking a moment to think things over, really listening, having good conversations, working things through from a team perspective, getting some help when things get tough, finding a middle ground, staying emotionally tough, and learning from the fights you go through, you'll handle conflicts like a champ.

# Chapter Thirteen
## THE FAMILY TRIBE AND THE SCHOOL SCENE

As a teen, you usually have two environments you are bouncing back from...the home front and school, plus the extracurricular stuff. You generally spend almost all of your time between those two zones, but they have very different dynamics. This in itself can be pretty overwhelming because you have to adapt to being a couple of different roles, a student and family member, etc. You are at school, around a ton of people, and all different types of people, too. You have your teachers, classmates, friends etc. A lot is coming at you. Then you go home and are dealing with family members. Sometimes you get along with them, and sometimes you don't. You are also dealing with your role and expectations there, too. I am going to give you some tips on how to handle your roles, your relationships, and interactions between these zones to help you sail a bit better.

## DEALING WITH PARENTS AND SIBLINGS

### FAMILY MEMBERS ARE PEOPLE FIRST

Let's first talk about the authority figures or the people who take care of you at home. One thing I want you to remember is that before your mom was your mom, your dad was your dad, and your grandma was your grandma; they are people first. This means they are human first. **The reason I bring this up is because when I was growing up, I only thought of my parents as parents.** I really forgot that before they had me, they had their own entire lives, their own experiences, their own thoughts, and they made their own set of mistakes way before I got into the picture. They didn't just plop down to earth as a mom, dad, grandma, grandpa, or aunt. They were a teen too, once, even though it was a different time. That came with all the insecurities, new people, changes, more responsibilities, and a lot of the dynamics that you are going through right now.

As a teen, I didn't really think about that. I MAINLY saw them as ONLY mom and dad. I didn't really see them as "human" like me if you know what I mean. I saw them as just a role. So if they made a mistake, I would think, "they aren't supposed to do that...they are older, they know better, they aren't supposed to be making mistakes. They are supposed to know everything". Well, the fact is, adults are trying to figure things out too. You may be the first teen they have taken care of. Or the first teen girl they have taken care of. Lots of things are new for them too. So what I'm trying to get at is, remember, the people who take care of you are human first, just like you, with all that stuff that comes with being human, like having emotions, feeling insecure or hurt, etc. So see your family members as people first, just like you, and not only their role. Be kind, empathetic, and understanding.

Also realize that the people who take care of you can offer a lot of guidance and perspective BECAUSE they have just been through some of the same experiences before lots of times. There is real truth that times have changed things, so some things aren't EXACTLY the same, but there are LOTS of things and experiences that ARE the same. They often have a bigger picture, been there, done that clearer view because they have lived many more stages in life. Respect that.

## DIFFERENCES ARE OK

**Another thing to remember is that, although you guys are in the same family, people can be VERY different.** This can especially be the case with siblings. If you live in a house with brothers and/or sisters, you can be so different from each other, right? Even though you guys grew up in the same home, the same neighborhood, with the same parent(s), you and your sibling(s) can have completely different personalities. In fact, I think siblings who grew up in the exact same house and environment tend to be more different than the same. That includes across all cultures, demographics and economic spectrum. Most of the time, people living in the same house become very different people.

**So, being part of a family, you have to recognize and accept those differences.** Respect the differences. If they don't like the same music you do, the same foods, to do the same things, it's OK. Lots of times, the differences can introduce you to new things and expand your world.

## GOOD COMMUNICATION

One thing that is vital everywhere and helps people get along, ESPECIALLY with your family, is good communication. Again, this is not just "talking"; it is about listening too. When you are open about what you're feeling and also listen to what your family has to say, things go smoother.

## WHEN YOU WANT TO TALK, PICK A GOOD TIME

When you have something you really need to sit down and talk about, pick the right time to chat. **Don't try to dive into serious stuff when everyone's stressed or super busy and running around.** They probably can't give you the attention, patience and even give you the answer you are looking for under those circumstances. Wait for a chill moment when you can actually talk without distractions or tension.

**When do you think it is a good time to fully discuss things in your house?**

_____

_____

_____

## WHEN YOU DO TALK, HOW ARE YOU SAYING IT?

As I mentioned before, try to use "I" statements, you know? For example, instead of saying, "You never let me do anything," try something like, "I feel some more freedom would be great." It's less about blaming and more about expressing what's up with you. Remember, blame games go downhill fast.

## ACTUALLY LISTEN WHEN THEY TALK. LIKE, REALLY LISTEN

Show you're trying to get where they're coming from. **It's not just waiting for your turn to speak but hearing them out.** This can make the whole convo way smoother and you might actually find some common ground solutions.

**If this isn't already part of your family routine, maybe suggest a regular time to talk about things.** Some families set aside specific regular times so everyone can hash things out that come up for the week. If you think this would be helpful to you and you don't already have this set up, then suggest some dedicated time when you can sit down and discuss what is on your mind.

**The reality is everyone in the house probably has their own thing going on between work, work drama, school, school drama, responsibilities, and everything else.** It is really easy to get stuck in your world. If you guys can set aside a focused, dedicated time with no distractions, where you can openly talk, and people are listening, it is a great way to reconnect, resolve problems, and support each other. **If you are worried that you will forget what you want to say when that time comes, I am always a big fan of writing things down.** That way, you won't be stressed about forgetting what to say. Write down everything you want to say when your time comes up.

## DEALING WITH SIBLING RIVALRY WITHOUT WORLD WAR III AT HOME

Handling sibling arguments without turning your house into a war zone is about setting some ground rules. **First off, make sure you both know what's yours and what's off-limits.** For example, if your brother's always borrowing your stuff without asking, lay down some rules. Respect each other's space and stuff, and try to find a middle ground when you have to share. Make an agreement that you both can agree to and be happy with. It helps to get your parents on board with agreed repercussions if boundaries are violated.

When you do argue, talk it out instead of just going off. **Be straight up about what's bothering you and listen to what they've got to say, too.** It is better if you guys work together to figure out a solution that doesn't end in a shouting match.

**Make an effort to spend some chill time together.** Do stuff you both like, maybe plan a family event or a game night, or maybe plan something with just you guys. It's not just about avoiding arguments. It is about actually having some fun together. Yes, YOU can get the ball rolling. When you're doing fun stuff together, you're less likely to get on each other's nerves. So, respect each other's space, work through the tough patches, and do something fun together. It can help the relationship.

## SHOW UP FOR THE FAM. BE PRESENT

*"Family. Today's little moments become tomorrow's precious memories."*
— *unknown*

**When it is family spending time together, show up and be present. Not only is it important physically show up but mentally show up.** Put down your phone and focus on your family time. I can promise you, as you get older, even though you may not get along with your brother now or think your parents are annoying, you will look back and cherish the family times you had together. So when there is a family dinner, movie night, watching a game, or just hanging out...show up and actually focus on spending time together. Also, keep an open mind on activities and even try to find common interests that you can do together. **Remember, people are happier when they have a great community around them.** Family is probably the most important part of your community. Doing stuff together is a great way to make some amazing, life-lasting memories and get closer to your family.

**What are some family activities that have been your favorites and why?**

_____

_____

_____

_____

_____

_____

**Is there something you want to do with your family that you guys haven't tried or wish you could do more of?**

_____

_____

_____

_____

## HOW TO HANDLE RELATIONSHIPS AT SCHOOL

Remember when I mentioned your parents, your grandparents were people first before they had that role? The same goes for your teachers. Most teens see their teachers as Mr. So and So, the math teacher, etc. They are human and people before they are teachers. **So, that means being respectful is the first step to getting along better with your teachers.**

It's basic, but it matters. A simple 'thanks' after they explain something can go a long way. Look them in the eye when you talk to them, smile, speak clearly, listen actively, and thank them for their time...the basic skills of good communication we talked about earlier.

**Also, if you don't understand something, say something. You are at school to learn.** If you don't get an idea or concept, don't just shrug it off. Ask your teacher for help. They're there to teach and will appreciate that you are taking your learning seriously.

**And in class, try to be more than just a face in the crowd.** Join in discussions, ask questions, and be part of what's going on. It shows you care about what you're learning. Teachers notice this stuff, and it can definitely improve how you get along with them. So, to recap... be respectful, don't be afraid to ask for help, and get involved in class. It makes a difference.

## CLASSROOM DYNAMICS

Handling things in class and during group projects is mostly about teamwork. Be respectful and inclusive to all your classmates and show support, whether someone's acing it or struggling a bit.

When you're in a group project, it's important that everyone gets to have their say. Listen to what they've got to share and try to figure out who's good at what so you can split up the work in a way that makes sense. Everyone's got their strengths, so play to those.

**What are some of your strengths during a group project?**

_____

_____

Sometimes, there will be conflicts, and you will hit some bumps with your group. **When that happens, keep your cool and talk it out.** Be straightforward and direct about any issues but do it in a way that's not about blaming or disrespect. Find a way to sort it out without making a big deal of it so you can all move forward as a unit and get all the work done. Be a team player, listen up, and handle any issues without the drama.

## DEALING WITH BULLIES AND HATERS

Dealing with bullies and the haters is tough and can be really traumatic. Pretty much EVERYONE has dealt with a bully at one point in their life. You would be surprised; people who you would think would be the LEAST bulliable and who other people see as perfect have actually been bullied at some point. I remember watching this boy bully this girl about being a "princess" when I was in the 6th grade. He called her names and made fun of her because she was too pretty and perfect. Yes, you and I are probably thinking the same thing. He probably had a crush on her, which is how he dealt with his insecurities. But the fact is, he was bullying her about this, trying to make her feel bad about herself because she came across to everyone else as perfect. It was a ridiculous scene.

Unfortunately, I also have to tell you that there will be bullies well past the teen years. Adults deal with bullies, too. The reality is that most bullies have been bullied themselves. They often turn that hurt into just becoming a jerk to someone else. It is a cycle to make themselves feel better because someone else made them feel worse. **It isn't about you.**

**But the most important thing I want you to remember is that what they say doesn't and will never define you.** You know who you are, and you are amazing. You are unique, caring, full of talents (even if you haven't found them yet, but you will), and have a lot of inner strength. You are going to do incredible things in life, and these bullies will be a long-faded memory that you can throw in the literal garbage. What they say has zero to do with who you really are. **So if someone puts you down, it is up to you to build your confidence up.** Hang out with people who lift you up, not tear you down. Do things that make you feel good about yourself.

**Stand your ground and be clear about your boundaries. You've got every right to speak up for yourself.** If someone's crossing the line, it's perfectly OK to say "no" and really mean it. And if things are getting bad or keep going, talk to someone about it - like a friend, a teacher, or a counselor, your parents. **You aren't telling on someone; you are taking care of yourself. You have an absolute right to take care of yourself.** So, believe in yourself, don't be afraid to stand up for what's right, and get help when you need it. **You don't have to deal with this stuff alone.**

**Listen Up Bullies. Beware...You May Bully Someone that Is Your Boss Later**

Dear Bully,

I can tell you so many stories about people who bullied people that later on in life regretted it because that very person ended up being a superior where they worked or had some other positions of power or even became famous. Some people may forgive you but some won't. Don't be stupid. Be nice and treat people with respect. Not only should you not be a jerk just because that is a terrible way to be in life and will likely ending hurt you...you just never know who that person will grow up to be. So for all obvious reasons, don't take your frustrations out on someone else. **You will be an adult far longer than you will be a kid.** Be kind, be respectful and live a life you will be proud of when you look back. Thank you.

**With much love, Your Future Self**

Chris Rock, the famous comedian, talked about a horrible bully he dealt with growing up. This guy used to throw him down the stairs, beat him up and call him the worst names through out high school. Chris said it was absolutely traumatizing. One day on set of a movie Chris was not only acting in but was directing (basically he was the boss of the whole production), he saw a security guard and recognized him as the same bully who used to throw him down the stairs. Chris talked about barely acknowledging him on set and thought this guy could have ended up being his friend he grew up with instead of a bully who tormented him. He could have been invited to the trailer, hung out, gone to parties with the rest of the crew, and exposed to a whole new world if he wasn't such a mean kid to him.

*Chapter Fourteen*

# MINDSET IS EVERYTHING

You see me writing about a positive mindset all over this book. This chapter recaps some of the highlights because I believe it is one of the most important skills to master to build lasting confidence and strong social skills. This is why the topic deserves its very own chapter. Out of all the topics, I think this is my favorite and most important one. Why? Because it is about how we talk to ourselves. **The longest, closest, and most important relationship will be the relationship with ourselves.** That means we have to learn how to talk to ourselves with positivity, kindness, encouragement, and support. **We have to learn to be our biggest cheerleader and best friend.**

How we THINK has a really huge impact on how we feel about ourselves. It is the foundation for everything else – our choices, how we handle tough situations, all of it. How you think, what you believe, and what you say to yourself often shape how life will go. **We're going to dive into talking to ourselves positively, shutting down the negative self-talk, and spotting beliefs that might be holding us back and dragging us down.** We'll talk about being kind to ourselves and always finding ways to improve because that's key to unlocking all the amazing things we can accomplish.

## ▌ POSITIVE TALK IS NOT JUST WHOO WHOO. IT CREATES REAL CHANGE

**There is no question positive self-talk can make you stronger, lower your stress levels, and even help you perform better.** Talking to yourself supportively is powerful, but many people don't get how important it is. The stuff we tell ourselves can really boost our confidence and overall mood. If we're constantly beating ourselves up, saying we're not good enough, or stressing over past mistakes, it just makes us doubt ourselves more. But, if we start flipping those negative thoughts into positive ones, we are actually rewiring our brains to be more confident.

## PAY ATTENTION TO YOUR THOUGHTS

To get in the habit of positive thoughts, you've got to watch out for those sneaky negative thoughts and kick them out. Sometimes, these negative beliefs come from old stuff, like things that happened when you were younger or what people around you say. Although having high standards is great, there are also unhealthy high standards you set for yourself (yes social media, I am calling you out). **But here's the trick: start doubting those negative beliefs.** Ask yourself if they're really true. For example, say that you didn't play as well as you wanted in a game. Instead of telling yourself, "I suck" or "I'm terrible,"... replace them with "I know I can do better," or "This is just an opportunity for me to improve." Replace them with solid, positive vibes. Think things like, "I've got what it takes" or "Every challenge is a chance to grow." Don't wait while you sink further into self-doubt. **Switch that thought as soon as it comes up.** Don't let those negative thoughts hang around. Doing this not only boosts your confidence but also makes you feel stronger when you're facing tough times.

## BEING NICE TO YOURSELF IS THE KEY TO HAVING A HEALTHY ATTITUDE

In a world where it feels like everyone's always telling you to be tough and compare yourself to others, showing yourself some kindness is a really big deal. Instead of beating ourselves up for what we think are our flaws or mistakes, we can choose to treat ourselves with the same kindness and understanding we'd give to our friends we cherish and close family members we respect. When we are nice to ourselves, we're building a deep sense of accepting who we are and understanding ourselves, even the not-so-perfect parts.

## FORGIVE YOURSELF IF YOU MESS UP

A growth mindset means you believe that you can get better at things and learn more if you put in the effort and keep trying, **even if you mess up along the way.** When stuff gets tough, or you face setbacks, people with a growth mindset see those obstacles as chances to learn and get better. You don't worry so much about failing, and you focus on the opportunities that come your way. With this way of thinking, you get tougher, more adaptable, and way more confident in your ability to handle challenges and reach your goals.

Just keep this in mind: your mindset is like the commander-in-chief of your life. The way you think, what you believe, and what you tell yourself shape how things go down. So be aware that we become what we think. Work on having a mindset that pushes you toward success and feeling fulfilled.

## Chapter Fifteen
# BALANCING ACT AND TIME MANAGEMENT

Balancing all the stuff on your plate and managing time is a struggle for teens and everyone with a busy schedule. Between school, friends, family, hobbies, sports, and even throw in the black hole of binge-watching marathons, it feels like there isn't enough time to get all the things you want and need done. Don't forget to add the alone time you probably need on top of all this. But don't stress out. Here are some skills that will help you manage your time better.

## BIG TASKS, LITTLE TASKS AND THE SCHEDULE

### MAKE A PLAN. HAVE A PLAN

I think you get that writing stuff down really helps organize your brain and life. Same with time management. **So, I recommend you get an organizational calendar app or a physical one to start the process of keeping track of your schedule.** Make sure you have one with an area where you can keep a lot of notes because we are going to start by making some lists.

### FIRST. THE LIST

List out ALL the stuff you need to do. There are going to be some big tasks and small tasks. I like the ones where you can just check tasks off when they are done. I also love the satisfaction of completing the tasks as a sense of accomplishment.

## SECOND: PRIORITIZE

Figure out which tasks NEED, MUST get done. Not all tasks are equal. Maybe put a big fat star by the ones that MUST get done.

## THIRD: TIMELINE

Make another list of the goals/tasks for the short and long term. Ask yourself what you want to accomplish today, this week, and this month?

## FOURTH: AFTER YOU HAVE A GAME PLAN TOGETHER, PUT THIS IN YOUR CALENDAR

The lists are there to write down and organize your thoughts. **Pick times when you can get your tasks done.** You can move around your tasks in the calendar if you need to, but at least you have them in front of you, so you know what you are dealing with.

For example, If you need your book report done in two weeks, input that "book report date" in your calendar. One by one, insert your timelines into your calendar.

## FIFTH: PUT YOUR OTHER SCHEDULED EVENTS IN THE CALENDAR TOO

Like your weekly tutor, your music lesson, your game, etc. Now, you can visually see what your day, your week, and your month look like. You can see in one snapshot of everything you have going on. **This will help you get a sense of how much time you are devoting to a task.**

## TIP #1: BREAK BIG TASKS INTO MORE BITE SIZE

**"Nothing is particularly hard if you break it down into small jobs."**

*-Henry Ford*

**If you have a really big task, it is always better to break it down into smaller steps.** That way, you won't get too overwhelmed by the BIG thing

130

you have to do (and dread). You also set a path on HOW to get the big task done. **Plus, smaller steps are just easier for the brain to understand.** We get less freaked out. Just take it one step at a time. So again, if you have a really huge task, break it down and write it down into smaller steps.

For example, if you have a big research report that you need to get done that is 25% of your final grade, then write the process out. The big task is to get the report done. Then, little steps are: pick a topic, find resources for the topic, create an outline, write the introduction etc. Remember, if you ever need help, don't be afraid to ask someone you trust for help!

**Write down a recent BIG project or task that you have to do or want to do. Then write down all the little steps you need to get that big project done.**

_____

_____

_____

_____

## TIP #2: BE REALISTIC ABOUT HOW LONG THINGS TAKE.

**The reality is MOST things take longer than you think** (on average, I would even say most things take about 33% longer than we think). Don't get caught in the trap of thinking, I can find all the resources I need for my report in 30 minutes, then I can run to my game, and then I can meet my parents for dinner. Over-scheduling and being rushed will cause you (and others) a lot of stress and frustration. **Just be real about time. You are saving yourself a lot of aggravation.**

## TIP #3: THE PROCRASTINATION MONSTER

This is one of those times you must be REAL and honest with yourself. **These days, it is just WAY too easy to get distracted.** If you know that you will get distracted by the basketball game on TV, then don't be in the same room as the basketball game. It is that simple. Just get all the distractions out of the way. Turn your phone on silent. Do what you need to do to get what you need done. As I said before, knowing yourself is a key step to leading a successful, fulfilling life. So, know what can take your attention away from your goals and get it off your radar.

**Write down some of your biggest distractions**

_____

_____

_____

_____

**Then write down the steps you need to take in order to move those distractions off the radar (or at least be less distracted)**

_____

_____

_____

_____

## TIP #4: FAM EFFORT

Get your family involved in the time management game. Think about even creating a family calendar so everyone knows what's going on. This way, you can avoid surprise chores or family gatherings that pop up out of nowhere.

# BALANCE

## TAKE SOME BREAKS AND AVOID ALL-NIGHTERS

Realize you can't be on the mission all the time. Schedule short breaks so you don't get too burnt out. When you are too burnt out, your energy gets low, making it harder to focus. Step away for a bit, chill out, do something else, and come back recharged. Whatever task you are doing will always get done better with a fresher look. And look, I know cramming all-nighters (or almost all-nighters) can happen once in a while, but they are brutal. Try planning ahead and instead studying in short, focused bursts. Find a quiet spot, ditch the distractions, and dive into your books for 25-45 minutes at a time.

## GIVE YOURSELF SOME REWARDS

When accomplishing a task (big or small), treat yourself to a job well done! Maybe your mom made your absolute favorite cake. Instead of eating it right after dinner, save it for the next day after finishing the intro to your research report. You can make this into a fun game. Think of rewards you can give yourself after completing something you want to accomplish.

**What are some rewards you think you can give yourself after accomplishing something you wanted or had to get done?**

_____

_____

_____

_____

# LEARN TO SAY NO

**"You can be a good person with a kind heart and still say no."**

_-Tiny Buddha_

133

You are human and can't do everything. **One of the most important lessons in life is to say "no" when something isn't right or good for you.** Don't try to people please your way through life if you end up sacrificing yourself in the meantime. It's okay to turn down things that don't fit into your schedule or don't work with what you want to accomplish. Think of it as avoiding unnecessary tasks that don't take you closer to completing your main tasks. This may not even apply to tasks. Maybe you just need some alone time to regroup in general. **Take care of you. People who care about you will understand.**

For example, a friend may text and say they want to hang out because they haven't seen you in a long time as they miss you. They are right, they haven't seen you in a while and you feel guilty. But you also have a huge school project that needs to get done STAT or maybe you had so many activities this week and you literally can't move. You don't want to hurt their feelings but going out wouldn't be the right thing for you.

**Convey this "no" with care and respect for yourself and them.** You can remind them although hanging out would be amazing, you have to get this project done or you must get some downtime for yourself. Most importantly, show them they are important by planning something ahead of time. "I would LOVE to see you soon so let's plan for something next week. How about Saturday afternoon?" or "what does your schedule look like next week?" This is a different message than "maybe another time" which can sound like a blow off. You are setting boundaries, taking care of yourself, and letting the other person know you care.

Let me give you a tougher scenario. Say your friend reaches out and invites you to hang out with some other people. One of those people is someone who tends to put you down, makes you feel uncomfortable or gets jealous and you always come away feeling bad. Although you like being with your friend, when you hang out with the other person too it never goes down well. You know deep down, saying no is the right thing for you.

**Be straight up and upfront** while respectfully telling your friend, "Hey, I love hanging out with you, but I have to be honest. When we're with Tammy there is usually drama, and it just ends up not being fun for me. I know you are friends with her, and I totally respect that but it's best for me to go out another time – hope you understand. Let me know when you're free!"

People in general (especially ones that really care about you) respect when you are being honest if it's done from a place of empathy because honesty takes courage. Honesty without empathy may just come across as venting. **If you show up for yourself while being considerate of the other person's emotions, it's a win-win.**

## STAY ORGANIZED

Organization is a slippery slope. What I mean by that is if you start letting things slide, it can just get stressful fast. So stay on top of being organized. The small amount of time you are taking now to be organized saves you big headaches and time in the future.

## GET SLEEP, EAT RIGHT, STAY ACTIVE

You can't do many things well, let alone think if you are tired, cranky, not rested, and not eating well. That is just a mess. Take great care of yourself! Recognize if you are running on empty. Not getting enough sleep and not being healthy are closely linked to depression. Lack of sleep changes the neurochemicals in your brain and can often show itself in your mood. In addition, you could have trouble focusing, learning, and reacting.

Science shows that being healthy and active releases "feel-good chemicals" like dopamine and serotonin in the brain.

But more importantly think of your mind and body like this. If someone told you that you only get one car for the rest of your life, how would you take care of it? Most of you wouldn't think about running it into the ground the first year. You would make sure you get it checked, take really good care it because it's the ONLY car you will have to get you around for the rest of your life. **Your mind and body is like that one car.** Start the habit of taking care of yourself early. **You only have one body, one mind. It's the only one you are ever going to have.**

## STAY FLEXIBLE

Keep checking how your plan's going. **If something's not working out, just change it up a bit.** Not everything will go according to plan the way you expected. That is normal. **Be honest with yourself if something isn't working, and figure out what needs to be changed.** If you need some help to figure this out, ask for it. Be vocal and get help if you need it.

## SOCIAL BALANCE

**Quality time always beats quantity time every single time.** Not only is it important to balance school life but also your friend life. Your friends can be your lifeline. They are the family you choose. Keep them a priority, but remember you don't need to be out all the time to have awesome friendships. Make the moments you have with them count. Find that balance that works for you.

## TECH BOUNDARIES

It is so easy to be sucked in by social media for hours, but we all know it is not the healthiest thing for you. **Set some tech boundaries for yourself.** Designate tech-free zones or hours during your day. That way, you won't fall down the TikTok rabbit hole. Even go on digital detox once in a while. Unplug, get outside, or read a book you have always wanted to start reading. You'll be amazed at how much extra time you suddenly have.

# HOBBIES, PASSIONS, AND THE PURSUIT OF AWESOMENESS

Make sure you leave time in your schedule to do things you love. Your hobbies and passions are what make you, well, you! Whether it's skateboarding, singing, cooking, or creating...it is really important to do something regularly that brings you happiness and joy. **BUT remember, with all the stuff you got going on, prioritize the ones you feel most passionate about**, and if you want some change, then rotate them. **Just don't spread yourself too thin and over-commit.**

What are some hobbies or passions you really want to keep making time for?

_____

_____

_____

_____

# Chapter Sixteen
## CHANGE IS GROWTH

Change change change. A lot of us don't like it. We don't know what exactly is going to happen after change. That's part of the problem...what comes after is unknown territory. As humans, we naturally don't like unknowns. What I can tell you for the most part, overall change is a good thing. And when you are a teen there is a lot of change. It is coming at you from all angles. Main thing is... it's important to know how to roll with it. Whether you're dealing with new roles, adjusting to different situations, handling surprises, or just growing up, seeing change as growth and potential life positive will open you up to a world of incredible opportunities. We're diving into why it's great to be open to change and giving you some real-life tips for handling transitions with confidence.

## GROWTH

Change is not just some annoying thing that messes up our routines—it's actually a key part of growing up. Change pushes us to leave our comfy zones, face our fears, and gain inner strength. When we're OK and cool with change, it's not just about being tough; it's also about seeing the world in a new way, grabbing chances, and turning into a different and better version of ourselves.

## GETTING USED TO NEW PLACES

When you're thrown into a new school, club, or crowd, it can be pretty scary trying to find your way around and make brand-new friends. But if you accept change in these situations, it's going to open up a new world. You learn about different parts of life, see things from different points of view, and get to meet some cool new people. So, don't be afraid to dive into change by trying out different stuff, making friends from different walks of life, and celebrating how great it is to be surrounded by new people. It's a chance to rethink what you know and get an intro to new ideas, which is a fun way to become a more well-rounded person.

## DEALING WITH BIG CHANGES

Change is not comfortable, but that's OK. There is a saying, **"people don't grow through easy times; people grow through change and tough times."** This is absolutely true. When things are easy, you aren't looking to change; you want things to be the same. But sometimes, change is exactly what you need to improve and take things to the next level.

But big changes are usually emotionally tough. **One of the best ways to handle them is by building a crew of people who support you.** Hang out with friends, family, or mentors who can give you advice, guidance, and some good pep talks.

Plus, when things are all over the place, it's even more important to take care of yourself. Make sure you're looking out for your head, body, and heart, and don't forget to be kind to yourself and cut yourself some slack as you navigate through these shifts. Find things that make you happy, take some time out for some self-reflection and thinking things over, and see these times as opportunities to grow and change for the better.

**What are some BIG changes that happened in your life that made you better at something or a better person?**

_____

_____

---

---

---

## HANDLING SURPRISES

Change usually comes with some real surprises, and knowing how to deal with them with the right attitude is a must. When you run into setbacks or roadblocks, have an " I can do this" view and look at them as chances to grow. Instead of getting stuck on what went wrong, focus on how you can fix things and what you can learn from the experience. As you tackle these challenges, you'll pick up some pretty useful and amazing problem-solving skills, get more creative, and become more flexible. You'll be super confident in your ability to handle whatever obstacles come your way.

## DEVELOPING RESILIENCE

Being tough means being able to bounce back from tough times with strength and a "not giving up" attitude. When you're really open to change, you're basically training yourself to be super tough. You are learning how to roll with the punches and keep going, no matter what life throws at you. You build up your toughness by looking at obstacles as chances to learn and grow, not as potential big failures. So, remember, being tough doesn't mean you avoid tough times—it means you face them straight on and use them to become even stronger and more awesome. Embrace change with confidence, understanding you will come out better because it's shaping you into a rock-solid, unstoppable force.

## REINVENTION

When you're embracing change, you're basically signing up for a personal growth adventure. You are ditching the comfort zone, seeing what else is going on, and discovering new sides of yourself. So, go ahead and dive into that new school and different hobbies, step up as a leader, or get into some volunteer action to challenge yourself and see what you can do. It's also about letting go of the past and knowing you're not stuck with just who you used to be. Change allows you to reinvent yourself, find new passions, and unleash your inner awesome.

*Chapter Seventeen*

# RAISE THE BAR FOR INTERVIEWS AND NETWORKING

When I was a teen, I had no idea how to interview or network, but I think it is such an overlooked skill to have, as many of you will start your journey into this new area soon. Having some basic skills will let you stand out and rise above the competition when trying to nab a part-time job, get that internship you wanted, or interviewing for college. I really do think there should be classes on this stuff as it's an essential skill that you will need throughout your life, so why not start early?

We have already gone through a lot of essential social skills that hopefully will become some of the basic building blocks for your interactions with the world. This also applies to interviewing and networking.

## ▎ GETTING READY FOR WHAT'S NEXT

Before you jump into your next social adventure, take a sec to do a little social self-check. Think about how you're doing with your social skills right now and where you could improve. Don't be afraid to ask for honest feedback— friends, fam, or mentors. Hearing from different people who care about you will give you a better view of your social skills, what you're great at, and where you can improve.

Knowing what you're good at and where you've got some room to grow is the foundation for improving as a person. Once you've got a better understanding of your strengths and areas to work on, you can set some real goals. For instance, if talking in front of a crowd is one of the scariest things you can think of, maybe it's time to sign up for a public speaking class to boost your confidence.

But here's the deal: it's not all about you – getting a handle on social skills affects your whole circle. Self-check and reflection are really important, but it's just as important to see what it is like from someone else's point of view. Being able to see things from other people's views makes it easier to vibe with other people. Being in touch with your own emotions, getting a good sense of how other people are feeling, and having the skill to manage both is absolutely essential. And trust me, this skill will be very helpful whether you're working, in college, or just doing your thing. You will be dealing with people day in and day out. When you get great at social skills, you set yourself up for strong, solid, healthy relationships, and handling tough spots like a superstar.

## SOCIAL SKILLS FOR NAILING JOB INTERVIEWS AND COLLEGE

So, one of the first big hurdles you'll tackle is nailing those job interviews or college interviews. And let me emphasize that having some solid social skills can really set you apart.

## FIRST: DO YOUR HOMEWORK ON THE COMPANY OR SCHOOL YOU'RE AIMING FOR

It shows you are willing to do more and you care about getting into the college or getting that job. This will also make the conversation go easier. **Also, instead of focusing on what YOU will get out of it when you get into the college you want or get the job you want, it is REALLY important that you explain what YOU bring to the table that will HELP THEM!** What will you add to the college campus that will improve the student body, or what skills and traits can YOU bring to the job that will help the company? **Explain WHY adding you will help them! That is what they really want to know about!** I can't stress this enough. Instead of focusing on the fact that you want a job so you have extra money to buy clothes, **it is much more important to convey how hiring/accepting you will help the company or the campus.**

For example, when interviewing for a retail job, you can stress how you have tackled any task with hard work. You are very prompt, reliable, and a team player. If you are interviewing for a job that has a lot of interactions with customers, you can stress how personable you are and how you love interacting with people. It is also advisable to add if you have any extra background that may be relevant to the job you are applying for. I would advise bringing great references to the interview (if you have previous employers or even someone with authority like a mentor or counselor). **The person interviewing you wants to know what they get if they decide to hire you or accept you.**

## SECOND: MAKING A GREAT FIRST IMPRESSION DURING THE INTERVIEW TAKES PRACTICE

Set up a time with some friends, family members, or a mentor you trust to practice what you plan to say during the interview. Get some feedback. Practice and talking things out helps you be less nervous when chatting with the person interviewing you. Bring your A-game.

## THIRD: DRESS APPROPRIATELY

"There is a saying: dress for the job you want, not the job you have." Considering that you are a teen, most of you will be going for your first job, so that saying may not make sense, but basically, it emphasizes, dress for the job you are applying for. This means making sure you wear something clean, neat, respectful, fits well, and appropriate for the specific job interview. If you need feedback about it, get it. Don't come in not put together, in worn out, unclean clothes and dirty shoes. You may not think people care, but people absolutely will. **They will look for details on who you are as a person and candidate by how you come into the interview.**

## FOURTH: KEEP AN EYE ON BODY LANGUAGE

Maintain eye contact, and sit up straight. Show confidence. Smile. Have a firm handshake.

## FIFTH: WHEN YOU'RE IN THESE INTERVIEWS, BE AN ACTIVE, CARING, ASSERTIVE LISTENER

Show respect and be polite. Be personable. Speak up and speak clearly. If you have further questions, ask them to clarify. Remember, just like you, your parents, your teachers, your siblings...**these people who are interviewing you are people first.** At the end of the interview, tell them, "Thank you for taking the time to speak with me." Be gracious. **<u>Good manners go a long way</u>**.

## SIXTH: HAVE SOME QUESTIONS PREPARED

After doing your research, having some already genuine, thoughtful, prepped questions beforehand for the person interviewing you shows that you are interested. It could be about the work or college environment, etc.

## SEVENTH: FOLLOW UP

**This may seem small, but it is actually significant.** Send them a thank you for the interview and for taking the time to meet with you. This will show you are grateful for the opportunity and display you have basic manners. It is respectful, polite, thoughtful, and shows initiative. All this goes a long way.

# NETWORKING

## WHAT IS NETWORKING?

**Networking is like making friends or acquaintances but for your future.** It's connecting with people who can help you learn about jobs, college, or just things you are interested in. And it's not just about getting a job but also sharing ideas, advice, and opportunities. Think about it as building a group of supportive people who can guide or help you figure out how to reach your goal or help you figure out what you want to do. It's making connections that might help you down the road.

## INTRO YOURSELF

When you meet someone who may help your future or guide you in some way, take the opportunity to introduce yourself; just start with a simple " Hi, my name is, and it is so nice to meet you. I would love to talk to you if you have a moment ". If they seem to have time, you can say something like " I am really passionate about (your interest)" and start a conversation.

## GET CONTACT INFORMATION

If you meet someone who is really interesting to you, ask them for their contact info. You can even follow up with a friendly email conveying how great it was to speak to them.

Be aware people are also dealing with busy schedules and just may not have the time to speak or meet further. That's OK. Just putting yourself out there is a great way to get the whole process going, and you never know where it will lead you.

## VOLUNTEER

If you are REALLY interested in something, look for events or situations where you can volunteer your time. It's a great way to learn extra skills, meet new people, and delve deeper into your interests.

Remember, like everything in life, interviewing and networking takes practice. The more you put yourself out there (and practice if it calms your nerves), the more comfortable and skilled you'll become.

Remember, developing unstoppable confidence and lifelong awesome social skills takes a lot of patience, time, courage, and internal strength. **But I believe in you. Shine your light.**

First. It is an intention

Then a behavior

Then a habit

Then a practice

Then second nature

Then it is simply who you are

I would love to hear your feedback and stories. If you want to reach out to me, you can email me:

nadia@pocketwisdomcompany.com

Your caring BFF ☺

**Nadia Walker**

Author and Founder of Pocket Wisdom Publishing

"The Savvy Teen" has been years in the
making and we hoped it you enjoyed it!

IF YOU LIKED
THE BOOK

Please Leave Us
A Review!